LAKTA MOON RISING

CONSTANCE GILLAM

DEDICATION

This book is dedicated to my children:
Damon, Jessica, and Whitney.

Always remember your ancestors. They endured much.

ACKNOWLEDGMENTS

A special thanks to Dr. Aaron Frith, Asst.Professor of History, and Laura Redish, Director of Native Languages of the Americas

CHAPTER ONE

Julia stood spread eagle, arms tied to each of the thick posts. She pretended the overseer wasn't standing behind her with a whip.

"One."

She pretended the swish of the whip was the wind whistling through the sugar cane.

"Two."

She pretended the groan that broke from her lips was the thunder building over the bayou.

"Three."

But the red-hot lash of fire that seared her flesh brought her back to the present. A present that blurred and swayed with the jerk of her body.

"Four."

The whip met her flesh again and fire spread from her shoulder blades to her fingers. Gray filled her vision. *Not gonna faint. Not gonna faint.*

Her head weaved and bobbed like a sunflower on a broken stalk. Once when she looked up, she thought she spotted Vincent, Mistress Donnelly's nephew. Why didn't he save her? Why didn't he stop Mr. Jack from whipping her?

She remembered the first time he took her. Afterwards as he wiped away her tears, he'd whispered, "Call me Vincent." Now he leaned against a cypress tree, a cheroot drooping from his lips.

He ain't gonna save you.

"Five."

Lord, help me. She tried to brace for the slash of the whip. The leather cut across her already open flesh. Her back arched. Pain speared through her gut and tore her in two.

Everything went gray. She didn't fight the darkness.

"Julia. Come on back, girl."

Her mama's voice. But…but her mama was dead. Had been since last winter.

Water flowed over Julia's legs, across her stomach and slid over breasts. So cool and clear. Strange. This time of year the water was warm and murky.

She put her head back and stared up at the sun. Not the hot, baking sun of August but the warm soft rays of March. She floated along on the current, imaging the dress Vincent had promised her from Paris.

Julia winced. The water had turned hot and pain cramped her body. Had one of those cottonmouths bit her? Her mama had warned her about swimming in the bayou.

"Come on back."

Who was talking? She couldn't see anybody on the shore.

Julia rolled onto her stomach, kicking her feet and using her arms like Bo had shown her. But she wasn't moving. Instead she sank below the surface. The dark depths of the lake weren't black but green. Something moved on the edge of her vision. A big fish. A big monster whose sharp teeth snapped at her. A fish that looked surprisingly like Mistress Amélie, Vincent's new wife.

"You ain't gonna die, girl. I taught you to fight." Her mama's voice soft but threaded with iron.

"Mama?" Julia stood. Her mother waited on the shore. Julia walked toward her. She didn't feel the stones under her bare feet, didn't feel the sandy soil between her toes, and didn't feel the heat of the ground. Strange.

Her mother moved further from the water and deeper into the woods.

"Mama, wait." Tightness like the chains from the whipping post crushed her chest. "Don't leave."

"Mama's got to go. But you gonna be all right. You got the blood of the Mandinka. You gonna be fine." Her mother turned and disappeared among the trees.

The dark, hot cabin smelled of greens and pork maw. Julia's innards growled. She lay on her belly, her face turned to the side. Every time she tried to lift her head, pain tore at her body like the lash of the whip lay into her flesh again. She sought relief in sleep.

When she woke again, a weak light filtered through the cloth that hung at the cabin door. The curtain let in the sun, the rain, the bugs and the occasional prowling man from the big house. Mistress Amélie never entered the slave cabins. But someone had planted her shawl in Julia's quarters. And why hadn't Vincent told his wife the truth? That Julia would never steal.

A big dark shadow blocked out the light.

Mr. Jack, the overseer, squatted on his haunches and peered into her face. His breath smelled of onions and rum. He ran a finger over her cheek. "Had to be all fancy and spread your legs for the Mistress's weak ass nephew. What did it get ya?" His eyes flittered to her back. "Fifteen lashes. I try to be as gentle as I could, but Mistress was watching from her balcony."

He lied. He'd meant to hurt her.

"Now that Mistress Amélie know about you and Vincent, I reckon he won't be coming down here." The overseer licked his thin lips. "So you and me gonna get acquainted."

She swallowed against the liquid that surged into her throat. Lil Gal had died a few months back after Mr. Jack had gotten acquainted—as he said—with her. The women whispered about how mean he was.

He leaned forward until the stench of his rotten teeth filled her nose. "Get well quick, 'cause you and me are gonna have some good times." He stood, lifted the curtain and was gone as quickly as he'd appeared.

Tears slid down her cheeks. She didn't have no time for tears. Tears wouldn't save her when he came around again, wanting what Vincent had thought was his due. Pushing up on one elbow, she attempted to get to her knees. Pain washed over her like a summer storm, sudden, violent and wet.

Someone stood in the cabin doorway, blocking the light.

"You all right, child?" It was old Bessie. Too feeble to work the cane anymore, she tended the babies and watched over the cooking pots. Her toothless gums worried a wad of tobacco as she reached out a swollen-knuckled hand and touched Julia's face. Without uttering a word, she shuffled to the table that stood in the center of the one-room cabin and scooped out water from the wooden bucket.

"Here." She held the cup as Julia drank. Some of the water managed to get in her mouth, the rest soaked the pallet.

"I saw Mama."

Bessie's face tightened up until it looked like a rotten pumpkin, all caved in on itself. She didn't say anything, only started to hum underneath her breath. Julia gripped the old woman's hand and squeezed. Bessie was her mama's older sister. They'd been lucky and been brought by Master Donnelly and never sold. Mama had been more to the Master than his cook and housekeeper. Julia remembered when he would visit her late at night. She would hear his grunts and groans from her pallet in the corner. Her five-year-old mind didn't understand what was happening, but she did later. Word was she was Master Donnelly's by-blow. None of that mattered now 'cause he'd died five years past, leaving the plantation to his wife's nephew,

Vincent DuRousseau. And Vincent did to her what Master did to her mama.

"You lost the babe."

Julia's eyes flew open. These past two months she'd missed her monthly but turned a blind eye to what that meant.

"You'll have more," Bessie said, stoking Julia's hair. "You young."

But Julia didn't want any more children, not like this. Not born into slavery and whipped because the wind blew from the west instead of the east.

"Rest now. I'll bring you some suppa later." Bessie hobbled out of the cabin, leaving Julia alone with her thoughts and her pain.

Three days later Mistress Donnelly had sent word she wanted Julia back in the fields. She'd worked in the big house once alongside her mama. But when the Master died, Mistress had put Julia and her mama out to work the cane.

Now, the August sun beat down without mercy on her weak body. She'd only been in the field for a couple of hours and already she was ready to drop.

She straightened and stretched her sore back.

"Heard you lost a babe." One row over, Hattie Mae also straightened from her stooped position gathering the stalks that had been felled by the men.

Gossip moved through the quarter like yellow fever, fast, vicious and deadly.

Julia ignored her. If the overseer caught them talking, he would take a whip to them both. She had had her fill of lashing. Plus, she didn't like Hattie Mae. This woman was evil walking.

Julia continued to bundle the fallen cane, the husk crackling under her bare feet.

"Edie says it's Massa Vincent's."

Julia didn't look up. She didn't have to. She could feel Hattie Mae's yellow eyes boring holes into her body.

Edie worked at the Big House, doing the job that once had been Julia's.

"Says Mistress Amélie hates your guts. It gonna be worse for you if she hears you carried his young'un."

Even though Julia had sworn never to bring a child into the world, the loss of this babe still twisted her insides. She gripped the edges of the cloth and tied a knot around the cane stalks. Lifting the sack, she tossed it over her shoulder. Pain sliced through her body like a blade cutting through dried stalks. She had been so caught up in trying to move away from Hattie Mae she had forgotten about her back. Now she stifled the moan that threatened to burst from her cracked lips. She would die before she let the other woman see her misery. It would give Hattie Mae too much pleasure.

Back ramrod straight, she stomped through the cane stalks toward the wagon. The sack beat her back like the whip had done three days ago.

"You looking mighty healthy, Julia girl." The overseer sat on the buckboard, watching her approach.

Her gut flip-flopped, threatening to bring up the hoecakes she'd eaten for breakfast. She knew what those words meant. He'd come a-calling tonight.

"I think she needs less strenuous work, Jack. You've just stripped the skin off her back."

Vincent, riding his horse Champion, came into view. The overseer's broad body had hid the owner of the plantation from Julia's sight. The roan danced restlessly beneath his master. Vincent tightened the horse's reins as he smiled at the overseer—a smile that didn't reach his gray eyes.

Mr. Jack's mouth thinned into a straight line, his normally red face flamed with more color. "She's working right fine, Mr. Vincent."

Vincent didn't answer just took off his straw hat and wiped the sweat from his brow.

As always Julia's gaze was drawn to the streak of white hair that started at Vincent's forehead and stopped at the crown.

"It ain't natural," Cook said, "for a man not yet thirty to have a patch of white hair only in that spot. Something must done scared the black out."

Julia didn't know how he'd gotten it and didn't care anymore. She blocked out the image of her fingers tangled in his hair. Stupid girl. Why had she thought he loved her? She was a slave—his property. He cared more for that horse than he did for her.

Under Vincent's watchful gaze, the overseer's nose opened and closed like the old bull in the south pasture just before it charged.

Vincent's smiled. His lips quirked in an upward motion that seemed to make the overseer's face even redder.

"Mr. Jack, where you want these extra stalks?" Bo, one of the elderly slaves, drew the overseer's attention. "No more room in this here wagon."

Bo, who'd been a strapping man ten years ago, now looked old and bent. He'd run when she'd been about five or six, and now his shoulders were bowed by the thick scars that had formed after the lashing.

The overseer stared down at the elderly man. He stared so long, the other slaves dropped their bundles of cane stalks and faded back into the fields.

Bo stood still under the overseer's study. Julia's heart hopped in her chest like a headless chicken. *Don't hurt him.*

"Julia. Go tell Josiah to bring up another wagon." This came from Vincent, who could have ridden Champion faster to deliver the message to the stable master than Julia could have walked. But she knew this was his way of getting her out of the overseer's sight.

She dropped her bundle. Gray Louisiana dust flew up around her. Turning on her heel, she trudged the half-mile or so to the main house and corral. The sun baked her overheated skin.

Vincent didn't fool her. He didn't care about her working in the field. He didn't want the overseer getting something he couldn't have. And Mistress Amélie had forbade him from seeking out Julia. She knew this because Cook, the only friend Julia had besides Bo, had heard the two arguing up at the big house.

Julia kicked a stone, ignoring the pain that shot up her foot. She wasn't a piece of meat to be fought over by two dogs in heat. But there was little she could do about keeping either one of them off her. She was property just like that cane swaying out in the field.

She stewed and gnawed so hard on that knowledge she missed the pounding of the horse's hooves until Champion was almost breathing down her neck. Startled, she stopped, shying away from the massive creature. She knew her eyes were probably as wide and white as the animal's. She hated horses, and somehow the beasts knew it.

Vincent dropped out of the saddle and pulled both Julia and Champion off the path into the trees.

Julia could barely breathe. He couldn't try to have her out here in the open, would he? His face sheened with sweat, and the vein in his throat beat hard as he pressed her up against a tree. The bark ground into her tender back. She bit back a groan.

The smell of his sweat strung her nose as his rapid breath sent blast of heat across her cheeks. She didn't dare look at him or protest as he touched his lips to hers. She fought not to respond, but her body had a mind of its own. Her lips parted under his coaxing.

Pain slice through her nether regions, remaining her of the babe she'd lost. She twisted her head, breaking the contact between their lips. With a hatred she didn't know she felt, she said, "I lost the babe."

Something spasmed across his handsome face. He and Mistress Amélie had no children after two years of marriage. Had he suspected she was with child? Did he even care? She almost laughed out loud. The baby would have been a slave. If it had been born, Mistress Amélie would have demanded it be sold.

He stepped back, turned sharply on his heel, and walked away. As Julia watched him ride off, she was glad the babe hadn't formed in her belly. No child of hers would be sold off like cattle. She'd kill herself first.

CHAPTER TWO

Julia sat in her dark cabin and waited until every candle had died out in the Quarter and waited some more. A storm brewed outside, kicking the wind high until the cane swished like the clash of machetes.

She'd been born on this plantation, in this very cabin. She'd live here alone after her mother's death because Vincent didn't want anybody to see his comings and goings. But his wife had found out. There'd been the stolen shawl found under Julia's mattress and then the beating. The beating Vincent hadn't stopped.

Bone and heart weary, she got up from the cabin's one chair. Moving aside the burlap that covered the window, she peered out into the night. Clouds hid the moon, making the path between her cabin and Bo's invisible. But she knew the way by heart.

Bo's cabin was the last one before the cane field. As much as she loved him, she'd hated to be around his place as a child because snakes slithered out of the field and sometimes found a home in his small room. With this in mind, she placed her bare feet carefully along the path.

She knocked quietly on his door. Not waiting for his invite, she slipped inside.

He snored softly on his pallet. She hated waking him because tomorrow would be a long backbreaking day, and he wasn't getting any younger. Kneeling on the dirt floor, she placed a hand lightly on his shoulder. "Bo."

He snorted and jerked.

"It's me, Julia."

Almost as black as night, his face was just barely visible in the dark room.

"What ya doing in here, chile?" His voice was gruff with sleep and fear. "Did anyone see ya?" He glanced toward the door.

She understood his concern. The overseer sometimes prowled the area seeking out whatever female had caught his fancy.

"I'm gonna run." Saying the words out loud gave truth to them. Sometime during the walk back to the Big House that afternoon, she'd decided.

The room was so silent she could hear rats scratching in the corner.

"Let me put my pants on so I can think."

She turned her back and began moving carved wooden pieces around on the mantel. For the first time she felt ashamed for bringing her problems to him. She wasn't a little girl anymore, bringing wounded birds and broken corncob dolls for him to fix. She wouldn't involve him in her problems. "I'm sorry, Bo." She made for the door.

"Wait, Julia." He placed a large callused hand on her shoulder and then pressed her down into one of the cane back chairs he'd built.

"Cain't tell you not to run. I sho did. It's hard. Hard on even a big strappin' man like me. On a wee girl… Well, it could kill you. And now…" He pointed to her back. "With your beating, you'd died out there in the swamps."

He sighed and ran a hand over his thick features. "Massa Vincent won't let you go."

She dipped her head in shame. So he knew about Vincent's nightly visits.

"And Mistress Vincent and the old lady," he continued, "They might want you gone, girl, but only if it meant money in their pockets."

"They plan to sell me, Bo." Her heart beat like a runaway horse. She was torn, as much as she wanted to be free, the plantation was the only home she'd known. "Mistress Donnelly because…"

He placed a hand on her knee. "I know. Since Massa been gone, Mistress wants you outta here. Massa Vincent been telling her, no."

Bo lifted a cup of water to his lips and took a long swallow without taking his eyes off her. He put the cup down and wiped his mouth with the back of his hand. "If Massa Donnelly had been a little more private like…"

Did he know?

"It's not like I look like him." Julia waited for the shock to flash across Bo's face. It didn't come.

He knew.

Instead a smile flittered across his dark features. "You your mama's girl."

And she was. Her skin was lighter than her mama's coffee one, her nose thinner and her hair had more curl than kink to it, but they had the same slender body with full breasts and the same broad cheekbones.

"She was a beautiful woman."

Mouth slightly open, Julia stared at him. How had she never guessed? He'd loved her mama.

He turned away, and it was her turn to touch his shoulder in comfort. With his back still to her, he patted her hand, his callused palm rough against her skin. "Your mother ran once."

Julia's breath caught in her throat. Keeping her voice barely above a whisper, she asked, "What happened?"

"He brought her back. Gave her twenty lashes and placed a leg iron on her. Removed it when she was with child. She didn't run no mo."

Grief shot through Julia's gut, bending her at the waist and making her knees buckle. She'd cost her mother her freedom. Her mother had stayed a slave because of her.

Bo's gentle touch brought her out of her misery. She straightened her shoulders. "If you don't help me, I'm still going."

He hadn't lit a candle, but she saw the reluctant nod. "I helps you."

"I'm going up North. To Canada." She hadn't the slightest idea how far it was to that region of ice and snow, but she heard talk of it. And it seemed the farthest reaches of the world away from Vincent, Mistress, and this plantation. "I figure you'd know the way."

"Don't knows the way…"

Julia's new found hope dropped to her toes.

"…but I knows someone in town who could help you."

Her spirits lifted and a smile spread over her face.

"There be a family named Sunderland. Live near the Baptist church off from the bayou. Got some connection to the Underground Railroad. You get there, you be fine."

Julia had never been away from the plantation. Not even for a day. The bayou she knew, but other than that—nothing. But she nodded as though all he said made sense. She couldn't let him see the fear. He might try and change her mind, or worst, decide to go with her. She couldn't risk him coming. He'd run once before. If he was caught while helping her escape, Mistress Donnelly would have him killed.

She couldn't have Bo's death on her hands. She'd escape without him. How hard could it be to find the farm at the end of the bayou?

Later, keeping to the shadows, she made her way back to her cabin, thinking of Master Donnelly's cruelty toward her mama. He'd always been good to her, well…as good as one person enslaving another could be. Had there been two men living in that body?

She let out a relieved breath when she stepped into her shack.

"Out kinda of late, ain't ya?"

Julia yelped and jumped a foot. The overseer's white face emerged from the darkness.

How long had he been there? Had he seen her leave Bo's cabin?

"Ah… I had to empty the slop jar."

"In the middle of the night." He glanced down at her hands. "Where is it?"

Stupid. Stupid. Stupid. "I…I dropped it down the hole." She laughed nervously. "I didn't want to go huntin' for it in the dark."

He didn't laugh but instead shortened the distance between them. Gripping her shoulders cruelly between his giant hands, he pulled her roughly toward his sweaty body. "You lyin' to me?"

Could he hear her heart thumpin' in her chest? "No, suh. I really did drop it in." But in case he'd been waiting a while, she added, "Too hot in here to sleep. I tried to sleep outside."

Something in her voice must have rung true for him, because he said, "Why'd you come back? It's still hot."

"Snakes."

He laughed and released her arms. "Yep. There be loads of snakes out in that cane. Big Henry got bit yesterday."

She'd heard. She'd also heard his leg had turned purple and swollen to twice its size.

Mr. Jack squeezing her breasts brought her out of thoughts of Big Henry. She didn't flinch or call out. If she did, he'd hurt her more. He loved to cause pain.

"You a mighty fine bitch. You know that?" His breath, smelling of rum, fanned her face. "Yah. Mighty fine."

Before she could blink his fingers snaked under her skirts to palm her between her legs. When he encountered the rags she used during her bleeding time, he jerked his hand out and grunted in disgust.

"Well, that's just dandy." He spat on the dirt floor. "I'll have to get a taste of that later."

He pushed aside the curtain and strode out the cabin. Julia sank to her knees. She had to leave. And soon.

Three evenings later Julia made her way toward the Big House. Not boldly—a field hand had no business at the House—but like a thief moving from pillar to post, keeping to the shadows.

Vincent had snuck into to her cabin last night. She told him her monthly visitor had arrived, but that excuse would only last a few more days. It was time to run, so she'd come to say her goodbye to the one person besides Bo she loved the most—Cook. Cook had been like a mother to her since her own mama had passed.

Julia waited until dinnertime. Cook's duties would be done, the house girls would be busy serving, and Vincent, Mistress Amélie, and Mistress Donnelly would all be dining together.

"How you feeling, girl?" Cook collapsed onto the bench Bo had built for her, rubbing her legs as she studied Julia. Cook's knees were swollen big as melons.

She tried to smile, but knowing this would be the last time she saw Cook brought tears to her eyes. Cook reached out and gripped Julia's hand between her massive ones. "Trust in the Lawd, child. Everything will run its course."

She couldn't tell the older woman it wasn't Vincent who'd brought her to tears, but that she was leaving her family and going off to God only knew where.

Little Baby, Hattie Mae's twelve-year-old daughter, burst into the kitchen all wide-eyed and long-limbed. "Mistress Vincent wants—"

Before she could finish speaking, Mistress Amélie flounced into the room. A perfume that smelled like a skunk preceded her. "Theez..." Her nose wrinkled. She held a white flowered dish in front of her like a chamber pot. At the sight of Julia, the woman's eyes flew open wide.

"What...What," she sputtered. She dropped the bowl, sending red sauce flying everywhere. "You—you whore, you..."

Jaw clenching, heart hammering heat flashed over Julia's skin. She wanted to wrap her fingers around Vincent's wife's white throat, but common sense won out. Dashing to the exit, she tripped over the brick that held the door open and landed on her butt. Mistress Amélie was on her before she could untangle herself from her skirts.

"Whore, whore..." She beat Julia with the soup ladle. Julia threw up her arms to protect her face. Blows landed on her arms and hands.

"You spread your legs and entice my husband. You bitch, you, you whore. "

Strangely, the one thought that went through Julia's mind as she curled in a ball against the blows was how many blaspheme words Mistress Amélie knew.

The blows stopped as quickly as they'd started. Julia peered out from the protection of her arms. Vincent had taken the ladle from his wife and held her in his embrace. She wept prettily into his chest as he stared at Julia's legs, bared in the fall.

"Get up from there, Julia." Mistress Donnelly had entered the room, her hoops rising and falling like the sails on a swamp boat.

Cook pulled her up from the floor. "Git," she whispered.

Julia turned to flee.

"Stop." Mistress Donnelly's voice boomed like a riverboat captain's. The sound bounced around the small, hot space. Julia didn't turn but stared at the evening sky that beckoned to her from the open door. Freedom.

"What are you doing here? You have no business in the house."

Her mind worked frantically for a reason that would satisfy the Mistress. The punishment for leaving the cabins and entering the Big House without permission was a lashing or a night spent in the stockade, whatever punishment fit the Mistress's mood. Why hadn't she thought of something before she'd come? Because she thought she wouldn't be caught. Sometimes she was a witless twit. Turning, she faced the Mistress, mouth open with a lie.

"Cane," Cook sputtered. "Needed cane to sweeten the puddin'."

Mistress Donnelly's lips tightened into a hard line. "One of the girls could have fetched cane for you. There was no need for this one to come to the house."

"She come after I sent for her," Cook said. "I knows Massa Vincent likes a sweet bread puddin'."

Vincent's eyes lit with humor. He knew Cook was trying to save her from punishment.

"Yes. Thank you, Cook. Ladies, let's finish our dinner." His gaze strayed to the broken stew dish and the shrimp lying among the tomatoes and okra on the cobbled floor. He glanced back at Julia and Cook as he ushered the women out. "You might want to start with another main course."

"Yes, Massa." Cook said this loud enough so the departing women could hear. Julia breathed a sigh of relief. At least now she'd have longer to spend with Cook without the worry of being caught.

Julia could smell rain in the air. The clouds, thick and heavy, hid the moon, making this a perfect night to run. She waited until sometime after midnight and then gathered her small bundle of skillet bread, pork fat and one withered apple she'd snatched from the kitchen earlier that evening. She placed everything into an oil skinned rag and secured it with her shawl, which she tied around her waist. She wore boots Bo had taken from outside Mr. Jack's cabin. They were too big but would protect her feet and legs against snakes swimming in the bayou.

After casting one last glance at her hut, she eased out into the night.

A hand covered her mouth, shutting off a screech that rose in her throat.

"Shh…" Bo whispered in her ear. He pushed her back into the cabin.

Her hand gripped her throat as though she could keep her heart from jumping out of her body.

"Mr. Jack," Bo whispered. "Making his rounds."

Why was the overseer out so late? Normally he'd be asleep by now.

Julia crept to the curtain. What if he came to her place? She glanced over at Bo, who crouched motionless in one corner. What if he found Bo here? Two slaves together after dark would raise a lot of questions.

"Go," she said. "If he catches you—"

"Not gonna leave you to the mercy of that devil."

Since her mama died, he'd watched over her like a guardian angel.

"Couldn't do nothing when he beat you, but by de Lawd—"

A horse whinnied outside the cabin, cutting the old man off. She quickly shucked her apron and toed off the boots. She then stepped through the curtain and out into the night.

"What you doing out here, gal?"

Julia didn't look at the overseer but kept her gaze level with his knees. His horse fidgeted as though smelling her fear.

"Gonna take care of my business," she stated boldly.

She waited a long heartbeat to feel the lash of his tongue or his whip. But only a chuckled followed. "Pot still in the hole?"

It took her a moment to remember the lie she'd told him the previous night. "Yes, suh." She slipped easily into slave speech, hoping he'd forgotten she'd once worked in the Big House. "I really did drop it in the shithole. Didn't have a mind to go rootin' in there."

"Go to it and get back here quick. You remember I've been good to you. Darkies have no business wandering the plantation at night."

She wished she could spit at his feet. As though letting her go to that stinking hole would make up for the fifteen lashes he'd given her a week ago. She rushed to the outhouse, held her breath as long as she could and then hurried out.

He waited for her.

"Goodnight, Mr. Jack." She didn't glance in his direction but scuttled into the cabin and prayed he wouldn't follow her in.

Sweat trickled between her breasts and down her back. What she'd give for a swim in the bayou. What she'd give for the days when her only worries were catching enough catfish for her and her mother's dinner.

After what seemed like forever, she heard the clip clop of the overseer's horse moving away from her cabin.

"You runnin' tonight, wasn't you, gal?"

She let her silence speak for her.

Bo let out a sigh that almost shook the shack. "You need to wait some days. He knows something's up."

She couldn't wait. Like a bloodhound in heat, the overseer would be back, and this time wouldn't be put off by her woman's flow. Tonight was the night.

"You're right. I should wait."

"Good."

She could almost see his shoulders droop in relief.

Her heart cramped in her chest at the thought of the worry she caused him. "Go to bed. We'll plan tomorrow night."

His bare feet moved almost silently across the dirt floor. Easing aside the curtain, he peered outside. Turning, he gave her shoulder a squeeze. This would be the last time she saw him, so she threw her arms around him and hugged him tightly. "Thank you."

He squeezed back and then slipped out into the night.

CHAPTER THREE

Julia's head thudded against the mud walls of her cabin. She'd fallen asleep. How much time had passed? Had she missed her chance?

She peered through the curtain. The blackness of night hadn't faded into gray. She still had an hour or two before dawn.

Before she lost her nerve, she crept out of the hut and made a dash for the shelter of the cane. She tried to move quietly, but her heavy boots made her clumsy. The shoes crunched the fallen stalks like a company of soldiers. Her goal was the bayou beyond the fields. She needed to lose herself in the twisted waterway before sun-up.

As a child she'd played, swum, and caught fish there and knew all the curves of the byway. But Mr. Jack also knew the bayou maybe even better than her since he'd had the time to explore all the channels. When she turned six she'd started working with her mama in the Big House. No more time to play.

She broke into a trot that soon had her breathless, scratched, and cut from the sharp edges of the cane. In the distance, she could hear the voices of the field hands ready to start the day. She moved faster.

Just as the sun crept over the horizon, she left the safety of the field and without looking back dashed for the woods. She thought she heard a shout behind her. She didn't look back, just ran faster.

She followed the twisting path of the bayou. Water lapped lazily against the bank and the air smelled of rotting fish.

She ran until her breath came in ragged, choppy gasps. Pain stabbed her sides like big sewing needles and her legs shook like pork jelly. Bo had been right. Her body was too weak. When she tripped over a big tree root, she just lay there, panting. Every time she rose, her legs trembled and folded beneath her. How far had she traveled? Glancing up through the bramble of trees, she tried to find the sun. It wasn't quite overhead, so she judged she'd traveled four maybe five hours.

She crawled the few feet to the water's edge. It didn't matter that the water was black and murky. At this moment, with her clothes dried with sweat and her tongue stiff in her mouth, the water looked wonderful and tasted better. She lay on the ground and listened to her heart thud in her chest. When she caught her breath, she promised herself she'd be on her way.

The earth trembled beneath her body. Her head jerked up and her ears strained to catch a distant noise. The baying of hounds. The sound skittered across her skin and tightened the muscles in her throat, until she couldn't catch her breath. Getting to her feet, she set off at a lope. After a few steps her legs crumbled beneath her again. She hit the ground hard, her teeth clacking together. In desperation, she dug her fingers into the hard packed dirt and crawled.

Bo had told her hounds couldn't track scent once the hunted was in the water. She was the hunted, and she meant to survive. At the water's edge, she slid into the bayou.

The water wrapped around her like a mother's arms, warm and relaxing. For one moment, she thought of giving in to the urge to stay on the bottom and watch the fish swim and the seaweed sway. But her desire to live was stronger than her desire to make the swamp her grave.

When she surfaced the baying sounded closer. She dog paddled, frantically looking for a hiding place. The low-lying branches of an overhanging tree tangled in her hair, and the tree's underwater roots snagged her dress, pulling her down into the watery depths. When she broke the surface again, she was in a hollow beneath the same tree. She pressed against the wet, muddy bank and listened to the sniffling and baying of the hounds just overhead. She silently sank below the surface until the water lapped against her ears and nose. Trembling with fear, she waited for the men and dogs to tire of the search and move on.

"She got to be somewheres around here," The overseer's voice rang out above the howling of the hounds.

"Can't you shut those damn dogs up so we can hear ourselves think?" This was Vincent.

Vincent was hunting her. Her stomach twisted, and she pressed her fist into the soft flesh of her gut to dull the pain. Of course he was. He might lust after her, but she was his property. How could she forget that?

Something moved in the corner of her vision. She turned her head.

Her muscles knotted in fear.

A snake, so dark brown in color it almost faded into the murky water, wriggled within arm's reach. She held her breath, fighting the urge to flee.

One eye on the snake and one ear open to the conversation above her, she waited to see who or what would strike first.

"Look at them," Vincent shouted. "They've lost the scent."

The dogs' whining and scratching made Julia's skin dance.

When the snake sank its fangs into her arm, she swallowed a scream.

"Henry," the overseer yelled, "you take three men and two of the dogs and double back.

Fire a shot if you see her. Mr. Vincent and me will take the rest of the hounds and go on up ahead."

Julia lifted her arm out of the water, gritting her teeth against the pain. Two holes the size of peas dented her skin just below her funny bone. *Tie a rag tight just above the bite.* Her mama's words came back to her. But she couldn't do anything until the men left.

The horses' hooves pounded, and the howl of the hounds faded into the distance. She prayed none of the men double back.

Unsure if one or two soulcatchers remained on the road above, she waited. Instinct and her mama's instructions about snakebites told her she needed to move quickly. She eased out of her hiding place and peered through the tree's roots to the path above. No one lurked around ready to pounce.

What now? She couldn't continue ahead, and she couldn't go back.

She swam as quickly as she could to the opposite bank and pulled her body out of the water. Her scalp ached, and her clothes were wet and heavy. She couldn't stay here. The dogs would lead the men back to this spot. Bracing against a cypress tree, she tore off the sleeve of her dress. Already her arm had swollen as tight as a ripe muscadine. Before she tied the strip of cloth above the bit marks, she sucked hard on the area and spat as much of the foul-tasting venom out as she could. She continued to suck until she grew lightheaded from the effort. After tying the cloth tightly, she took off through the woods on a path between the one Mr. Jack, Vincent, and Henry had taken. She wanted to run, but her mama's words rang in her head. *The faster the heart beats, the faster the poison works.*

It wouldn't take them long to find her once they realized she hadn't circled back or wasn't up ahead. And at this pace, they'd find her quickly.

Branches slapped her face, and insects made a meal of her body as she trudged through a tangle of briars. Her clothes soon dried as the sun rose higher in the sky. Midday came and went. She grew lightheaded and dry-mouthed.

She wanted to eat, but somewhere in her escape she'd lost her food. The fish at the bottom of the bayou were probably feasting on her meal.

She didn't have time to dwell on her empty stomach or her throbbing arm. Pushing aside a mess of branches, she stepped into a clearing. Standing still, she tried to take in the place. A twig snapped. She spun around, took two steps back and found herself flying into the air.

She swallowed a scream as the world spun round and round.

Leaves and branches scraped her face.

So hot.

She pulled at the buttons of her dress.

Burning.

A mutter of voices. Strange words.

Silence. A sharp pain in her wounded arm. Stones held her eyes closed. Something cool on her forehead... A powerful stench filled her nose. Bugs landed on her body. She tried to shoo them away, but her arms wouldn't move. Bumpy motion.

Fingers forced her mouth open. Water trickled down her throat. She groaned when the water stopped. Wanted more. She tried to speak but could only croak. A hand covered her mouth. A hand that smelled of earth.

She dreamed.

The plantation. More lashes.

Bo and Cook. She smiled before drifting away again.

Julia's nose itched. Her face felt cooked and the strong smell of hay and sweat filled her nose. She sneezed.

Her head bobbed to the clip-clop of...of an animal's steps?

Her eyes flew open.

She was face down on the back of a moving horse. And between the thighs—

She twisted her head until she stared into a dark face with a big beak of a nose. A braid of black hair rest on each naked shoulder.

Her heart tried to claw its way out of her chest. She tried to scramble off the animal, but the male's cruel grip kept her planted firmly on the horse's back. Fear was like a rat gnawing at her innards.

She bucked and kicked. The animal neighed, dancing in circles.

The dark man spat out strange words. Julia wasn't sure if she slid off the horse or was pushed. She landed with a thud that rattled her teeth.

The horse reared up, powerful front legs pawing the air. Julia scooted out of range. The bronze man fought to control the animal.

He spat out more strange sounding words.

Five other Red Men—Injuns, Bo had called them—halted their horses and said something in their language to her rider and then laughed. He barked out words. They stopped laughing and galloped away.

She stared at the horse—black with white feet.

"Champion?"

At the sound of her voice, the horse turned his head toward her and whinnied.

How had this heathen gotten Vincent's horse? He wouldn't have parted with it for no amount of money.

The red man reached into his pouch and pulled out something he held up for her to see. A thatch of rich black hair with a wide white streak running through it.

She fainted.

Julia lay on the ground beneath a pine tree. Somewhere a horse snorted.

It all came back, Champion and the—the...

Vincent.

Her innards jumped into her throat. She turned her head and puked.

When she finished, she wiped her mouth with the back of her hand. Best not to think about him. Best to think how she was going to get away from these red men.

Bo had told her about these people. These Injuns. How they painted their faces and scalped women and children. It had seemed like just a story. A story that didn't touch her. She'd had her own worries. The overseer didn't take scalps. He just whipped the skin off your back.

She rose slowly, cradling her arm against her body.

The black sky was melting into gray. Birds called their morning song. Dawn approached. Five lumps sprawled on the ground. One was missing. Somewhere out there a sixth Indian lay in wait—ready for trouble, ready for her to make a run for it.

She settled back on the ground and closed her eyes and pretended to sleep. She touched the place where the snake had bit. The skin was tender but not painful. Her fingers came away greasy. She brought her fingers to her nose. Whew. Vile. The Indians had doctored on her arm. Why? Why hadn't they scalped her?

Tears pricked her eyes. Stop it. Why was she crying? Vincent wanted to capture her and take her back to the plantation—back to slavery. No. She wouldn't feel bad about his death.

She wrapped her arms around her body and let sleep take her.

Hook Nose kicked her awake. They traveled swiftly with her riding behind him, her arms tied around his waist. They stopped only to refill their drinking pouches when they neared water. No one spoke. They used hand signals only.

Once when she thought she heard horses, the party moved deeper into the woods and stopped, still as deer.

White men rode passed, close enough for her to reach out and touch. She didn't. Whites had already proven she was only important for working or bedding to death. If it was a choice between two devils, for now, she'd choose the red man. When the time was right, she'd run.

The right time came the next night. All six were asleep. No one kept watch.

As she crept toward the horses, her legs shook like green shoots in a summer storm. If she didn't get away now, she'd suffer the same fate as Vincent.

If she could just mount one of the horses without waking up the men, she'd be away.

Champion whinnied. Pushing her fear of horses deep down, she gripped the animal under his chin and attempted to lead him away. He was as stubborn as a jackass. "Come on," she whispered. He threw back his head to whinny again. She clamped both her hands around his muzzle and then backed out of the shelter of the trees, pulling the horse with her.

A hand twisted in her hair, pulling upward until her toes barely touched the ground. She pawed at the muscular arm. The hand tightened until the stars in the heaven flashed in front of her eyes. She prayed, waiting for a knife at her scalp or at her throat. Before she could complete her prayer to the Lord Almighty, the Indian flung her into the brush. She landed like an animal carcass among the briar. But her hair was still attached to her head.

She lay there, hoping they'd ride on without her. God was not going to be merciful to her this day. Five braves rode past her on their ponies. The sixth, Hook Nose, her personal captor, leaned down and snatched her up almost tearing her arm it from her shoulder. He plopped her on the horse behind him. Clasping her hands in front of him, he looped a rope around her wrists. Julia smacked into his back with a teeth-snapping lurch, as they raced to catch up with the others.

They traveled all day, stopping twice to water the horses. Her captor thrust dried rank-smelling meat into her hands. When she refused to eat, he took it and placed it back in the pouch at his waist. Many hours later, she ate the meat greedily.

They traveled hard, skirting outlying farms. When they stopped, Julia could hardly stand. Her legs trembled and her thighs burned. Leaning against a tree, she'd watch as the men squatted in the dirt drawing pictures she didn't understand.

With a face that looked like the butt end of a cow and a nose like an eagle's beak, her captor was the tallest of the six men and obviously the leader. His greasy black hair hung to his shoulders and blew in Julia's face when they galloped. The men wore animal skins to cover their male parts and all smelled of animal fat left too long in the sun.

One of the men showed her how to rub down the horses and prepare them for the night. A rope was tied around the forefeet of the animals. She assumed this kept them from wandering. She wasn't tied up but allowed to fletch water for the horses at whatever creek they camped near.

But the men watched her. Their gazes followed her every move. At night she slept lightly with a rock clutched in her fist.

Julia's head jerked and bobbed every morning from too little sleep. Even Champion's galloping gait couldn't keep her awake.

One morning, maybe seven days after her capture, she woke when the horses came to a stop.

A lone cabin sat in a clearing.

Heart lodged in her throat, she could barely swallow. Would these people help her? Her shoulders slumped. Why would they? They were white folks. They'd only turn her over to Mistress Donnelly or keep her for themselves. But if she stayed with these Indians, what would happen once they grew tired of her?

Off to the side of the cabin, split rails corralled in three horses.

Hook Nose shouted.

Champion shot out of the woods. Julia's head whipped backwards. Only being tied to her captor saved her from falling off the rear of the pony. The five braves whooped and hollered behind them.

Stirred up by the shouts, the horses in the corral no longer pranced but ran in wild circles. The flap over the cabin's window raised a fraction and the barrel of a shotgun appeared.

Three of Hook Nose's companion's shot arrows at the cabin while the fourth leapt off his pony and ran full out toward the corral. He opened the gate and shooed the horses out.

The cabin's door opened. A scrawny, bow-legged man charged out, rifle at the ready. "No, God damn, ye." He fired at the Indian chasing the horses away, missed and fumbled trying to jam another bullet into the gun.

Hook Nose released an arrow from his bow that caught the farmer full in the chest. His legs folded. He hit the ground, bounced once and lay still.

A skinny boy with hair straight as a cow's tail flew out of the cabin. "Papa."

From inside the farmhouse, a screeching wail raised the hairs on Julia's neck. A woman with one long thick braid stumbled out of the cabin and tried to pull the boy back inside. He shoved her away and ran straight for his father.

Hook Nose untied the rope that bound Julia's body to his. He jumped off his horse and ran full out toward the pair. Julia's breath caught in her throat. "Please, Lord, no."

She slid off the horse, taking a halting step toward the madness. Before she could blink, he'd grabbed the white woman's hair and slit her throat from ear to ear like bleeding a hog. A stain bloomed at the neck of her dress, changing the gown's color from a faded pink to bright red.

When Hook Nose put the knife to the woman's corn-colored hair, a gush of sour fluid filled Julia's mouth. She dropped to her knees and heaved, tears and spit mixing together.

The other Indians rode back into the farmyard herding the farmer's horses in front of them.

Raising the woman's scalp still dripping with blood over his head, Hook Nose let out a hooping shout. His men took up the cry and then galloped around the now orphaned boy.

Hook Nose turned his attention on the farmer's son, knife at the ready.

"No." Julia screamed. She jumped up and started to run. Her skirt tangled between her pumping legs. The distance between her and Hook Nose seemed to grow and grow. Unaware his life was about to end, the boy cradled his father's body.

"No." Julia shouted again, and she leapt on Hook Nose's back. Locking her arms around his neck, she reached for the arm that held the knife. Her strength was nothing to his. She tried with everything in her body to get the blade away. He only laughed as he turned in circles. Dizzy, she locked both hands around his neck. Realizing she was not strong enough to get the knife out of his grip, she leaned forward and sank her teeth into his ear. Warm, salty blood gushed into her mouth.

Hook Nose howled and then slammed the back of his head against her face. White flashes of light bloomed behind her eyelids. She slid off his back like a sack of grain off the back of a livery wagon. The inside of her mouth tasted like a coin she'd swallowed as a child. She couldn't draw breath.

She rose slowly, shaking her head. If she lived, she'd take inventory of her pains later, now she had to save the boy. She would not have this man-child's death on her conscience. She stumbled toward Hook Nose.

Hook Nose laughed as she lurched toward him. Julia could hear the laughter of the other men as she fought to stay on her feet.

Please, Lord, help me. Help me save one life today.

The boy hadn't moved. He stared off into the distance. Maybe this was a blessing, the Lord's way of sparing him the ugliness of losing his family.

The Lord didn't hear her prayer. With a jerk of his wrist, Hook Nose slit the boy's throat. Julia backed away, tripping over her skirts. She stumbled away. Let them shoot her in the back. She was past caring. She'd seen more violence today than she'd seen in all her sixteen summers at the Donnelly plantation.

The cool woods beckoned her, promising a relief from the horrors she'd witnessed. The river that ran alongside the farm called to her. She could sink in the murky depths and let the water be her grave. She'd fled one living nightmare only to find another.

But she couldn't give up. She was closer to freedom out here in the wilds than she'd ever be. Scooping up her skirts, she ran. If she could make it back to the woods, she would be safe. She could hide and wait for Hook Nose and his braves to tire of looking for her. Even though they were far from the bayou, she could almost smell the scent of the water—the rot, the damp earth. Just a few more steps—

Strong arms scooped her up and deposited her on the back of a horse. The stench of blood rose off Hook Nose like the smell of rotting fish. She tried to lean away from his body, not wanting to touch death, but he kept her hands firmly gripped in his. The blood of these people stained her skin as surely as *she'd* killed them.

CHAPTER FOUR

Julia rode numbly behind Hook Nose as his band traveled fast. During the day Julia took in the natural beauty of the land—animals that dug holes in the ground and barked, grey and white dogs that slinked through the underbrush. But at night the images of the boy and his mother without their scalps came back to haunt her.

When they stopped for the night, she cared for the horses, skinned small game and gathered water. Someone was always close at hand, watching. Would she ever be as free as the animals that raced across the land?

Late on the third day after leaving the farmhouse, they camped near a river that stank of rotten eggs. Julia wrinkled her nose as she gathered water to give to the horses. As much as she hated the smell, this might be the only water for days. She scooped some into her palm and drank it carefully. It tasted as bad as it smelled, but her stomach didn't cramp. As she took another sip, she studied her surroundings. The trees almost reached the sky and in some places blocked the sun with their green leaves. The water, though foul smelling, flowed rapidly over hidden boulders in the stream. Sunlight sparkled on the river like dancing fireflies.

She rose, stretched, arching her back to ease her sore muscles. The hairs on her arms and neck quivered.

She froze.

Across the stream, a band of Indians sat straight and tall on their ponies, watching her. How long had they been there? Rooted to the spot, she didn't know whether to flee back to camp—not that she believed Hook Nose and his band would protect her—or hide in the woods. When the first horse galloped into the river, she took flight.

When the band of ten entered the camp and dismounted, Hook Nose grasped the hand of the leader and the two pounded each other on the back. With hand gestures Hook Nose invited the guests to seat themselves around the campfire.

For the first time Julia realized there were different bands of Indians. Like there were different white people.

Once a riverboat had stopped at the plantation and a family had walked up the road from the river to the Big House. Mistress Donnelly's face had twisted into a frown. She'd called them Irish. The Master had invited them to stay a few days, much to the mistress's displeasure.

One of Hook Nose's men shoved Julia and gestured for her to gather more wood for the fire. The new arrivals had brought a deer.

"I'm not workhorse," she muttered to herself as she struggled to skin the large animal as the men sat around the fire and shared a pipe.

As she tended the meat over the campfire, she was aware of the stares from the new Indians. She kept her head down. She wanted to leave Hook Nose and his bloodthirsty ways, but she was wise enough to know she might be jumping from the kettle into the fire.

When her duties were done, she went to her sleeping spot. She woke sometime in the middle of the night to a hand on her breast. Scrambling out of her nest of pine needles, she tried to put as much space between her and this man. It was one of the Indians that had arrived this afternoon. Several men had gazed at her through the evening, but this one had followed her to the river and watched as she filled the skins with water. He hadn't approached but only stared at her boldly.

She didn't scream. Hook Nose wouldn't come to her rescue. After the blood bath at the farmer's cabin, she was surprised he hadn't slit her throat as she slept.

This Indian grunted once, stood and went back to his blanket. Julia sat upright, back against a tree the rest of the night, watching and waiting.

She woke to the sun peeking over the horizon. Hook Nose and his band had mounted their horses. She rose swiftly, brushing the needles from her stained and torn dress and made her way toward him. When she attempted to mount his horse, Hook Nose kicked her away. He pointed from her to an Indian that squatted near the banked fire—her attacker from the previous night. Without a backwards glance, Hook Nose galloped off. His band followed.

Julia stood in the dust kicked up by the horses, unsure what to do. She'd been with Hook Nose for seven long bloody days. He and his men had been brutal to her, but she knew what to expect. Would these new Indians treat her better or worse?

Rising from a squat at the now smoldering campfire, the Indian mounted his horse—a dark sleek animal with a black mane. From the herd, he selected a calm-looking pony. He brought the animal to Julia and gestured for her to mount.

She looked from the rope lying in the dirt to the departing Indian.

"I can't ride," she shouted after him. The Indian never turned around. The horse snorted and, trailing its reins, moseyed away. It munched grass, its tail swatting at big black flies.

The other Indians took little notice of her as they rounded up their wild horses. They surrounded the ponies and with a loud whoop herded them off.

If she was ever going to escape, she'd just been handed her chance at freedom. Having had her foot broken as a child by a horse's hooves, she carefully picked up the rope out of the dirt. At least, the Indian had put a cord around the animal's neck.

She led her horse over to a boulder. She dropped the rope and bunched her skirts around her thighs.

Working in the cane fields had made her legs strong, and she used those muscles to climb onto the rock. Once there, she swung a leg over the pony's back. He moved and she almost slid off the opposite side. At the last minute, she grabbed the horse's neck and held on until she could right herself. The rope still lay in the dust. She leaned forward, gripped the rein and tightened her thighs around the horse the way she'd seen Hook Nose do. The animal only turned his head, looked up at her with one huge eye, blew air through his nose and then continued grazing.

She stared after the departing Indians. How long would it be before they realized she wasn't trailing behind them?

"Come on, horse," she shouted. Her voice cracked.

The pony didn't respond.

Vincent had loved horses. She didn't know why. They were big stupid beasts. Yes, they could carry large loads, but they were still stupid.

Ignoring the flies that buzzed around the pony's neck, she crooned in its ear, "Come on now. We got to work together." She straightened and flicked the rope. "Let's go."

The animal lifted its head from the grass and slowly trotted after the other horses. "Not that way," she gritted through her teeth. She pulled back on the ropes, turning the animal's head in the direction she wanted it to go. That only resulted in the animal trying to bite her leg.

"Listen—" she almost called it a stupid beast but bit back the words in time. Her mama had always said you could catch more flies with honey than with vinegar.

"Come on, you can do it." She didn't know if she were talking to the horse or to herself. She pulled on the rope, turning the animal's head away from the Indians disappearing in the distance. This time she tightened her thighs around the horse and said, "Let's go," with the thunder she'd heard the overseer use.

The horse began to trot. She wanted to shout with joy. It wasn't a gallop, but at least they moved in the right direction.

When she heard hooves pounding the ground behind her, her heart did its own pounding, right into her throat.

She didn't turn around, just whipped the rope to and fro and jumped up and down on her horse's back to make it gallop. It didn't gallop.

She jumped off the beast, stumbled, then leapt to her feet and ran. She'd not be anyone's slave—ever again. She could almost feel the other horse's breath on her neck as her legs pumped. If she could just reach the trees, she could hide. She kept her eyes fixed on the woods. Almost there. A blur of motion and the Indian who'd grabbed her breast raced past her. He turned his horse, trotted back and scooped her up.

Fury and fear made her a demon woman. She lashed out, clawing any part of him her fingers could reach. When she scratched his face, he backhanded her. Like lightening, fire flashed from her jaw into her head. Her vision clouded to gray.

He tossed her across the horse's midsection.

"Please let me go." Tears filled her eyes, making the ground shift and shimmy.

The pony took off. Julia's head bounced against the animal's side with its every footfall.

After two days travel, they arrived in a village. Cone-shaped shelters—that Julia later learned were teepees—formed a circle around large fire pits.

The Indian who'd touched her, she called him Greasy Hair, took her to the teepee of an old gray-haired woman with rotten teeth.

He tied a rope around Julia's ankle and attached the other end of the hemp to a stake in the dirt outside the old woman's shelter. The day was windy and cold. Ash flew into Julia's eyes and hair as Greasy Hair and the woman shouted at each other. He stomped around Julia, gesturing wildly from her to the old woman. The old hag was not happy. At one point she spat on the ground by Julia's feet.

Finally, Greasy Hair stalked off.

One day faded into another with Julia grinding corn and roasting meat. She did all this while staked like an animal. The rope—which caused a bloody, weeping sore around her ankle—was long enough to reach the cooking fires but not long enough to outrun the old woman and her whip.

At night she bedded down on the opposite side of the teepee from Gray-Haired Woman and Greasy Hair. He had tried once to get onto Julia's sleeping mat. She'd put up such a fuss the woman, his mother Julia learned, woke. She kicked and beat both her son and Julia until the young man fled the tent.

One evening out of the red haze cast by the setting sun, an Indian party of fifteen or so galloped into the village. In their midst was a white woman. Hands tied together in front of her, the woman rode with a straight back and a vacant stare into the midst of curious Indian women.

She had hair the color of a sunset and a dress that once had been fine muslin. Julia knew this kind of woman. Like Mistress Donnelly, she was a gentle-born woman who'd used a parasol to protect her skin—skin that now looked like it had been cooked over a campfire. Hauled off her horse, she was handed over to the women who shared the tent next to Gray-Haired Woman.

"Wonder how long she's gonna last," Julia muttered as she turned the rabbits over the flames. Gently reared white women had slaves to do for them. This one would now be someone's slave. Would she adjust to her new world?

Gray-Haired Woman shrieked something, just before she beat Julia across the shoulders with her whip. Julia couldn't understand the words, but the meaning was clear. She gave the rabbits one more turn on the spit. Then she picked up her bowl and, using a stone, went back to grinding corn.

The following morning the females in the next teepee brought out the white woman. They didn't tie a rope around her ankle but left her sitting outside the hut alone while they went to the river. One look into those vacant eyes and Julia knew the woman's mind had fled. She'd seen things her soul couldn't tolerate.

Her clothes were torn, and blood soaked the once fine dress. Her glorious red hair had been hacked and stuck up in uneven batches over her head like a mangy gopher.

If she couldn't cook, skin, or take care of the horses, she wouldn't last long. The Indians would kill her. Why had they brought her back to the village? Why hadn't they killed her out on the Plain?

When Gray-Haired Woman went into the teepee for her afternoon nap, Julia shuffled over to the next tent. She squatted on her heels and looked the white woman in her face—something she would have never done on the plantation. But here on the Plains, hundreds of miles away from their previous existence, the violence of their current lives had made them equals.

"You wanna live?" she whispered to the white woman.

The woman didn't react but stared over Julia's shoulder. Julia shook her. Still no reaction.

"They're going to kill you as sure as you're sitting here. You'd better wake up."

The woman had beautiful blue eyes, the color of the sky but as empty as a cloudless day. Julia stared down at the soft hands now covered with insect bites and dirt.

Why was she doing this? This woman's kind had beaten her, sold off her friends, and had no guilt about using her in any way they wanted. But Julia knew why she sought to bring this woman out of her daze. To give up on life seemed so wrong. Life was too previous to just let it slip away.

She'd seen more of this beautiful country tied up on the back of a horse than she'd seen in all her sixteen years.

When the white woman didn't move or utter a word, Julia said, "So be it," and shuffled back to her teepee to stir the hominy cooking over the fire.

Her thoughts kept coming back to the white woman. Who was Julia to say this wasn't the way to end life? She'd sought freedom and what had it gotten her? She'd run away from the plantation to be enslaved on the Plains. Maybe she wasn't meant to find freedom. God had been cruel to allow her to flee only to be enslaved again away from the people she'd loved.

She glanced down at the rope that bound her to this existence. Her blood stained the hemp. How long could *she* continue before giving up? Maybe the white woman had the right of it. Maybe she was the lucky one.

Suddenly the ground shook with the force of what seemed like a hundred hooves. She whirled around to see a wall of men on horseback crest the hill and stampede toward the village. Julia sprang to her feet, her heart pounding in time to the thunderous sound. She and the white woman were right in the horses' path.

The horses' hooves churned up dirt as the warriors galloped like demons into the village.

Her fear made her clumsy, and the rope kept her from moving fast. She shoved the woman into her teepee just as the first horses reached their shelter.

Something hard knocked the air from her lungs. The earth rushed up. Her chin hit the hard packed dirt. Pain shot up her face. The hot breath of the horses scorched her neck.

Hooves landed all around her. She closed her eyes and waited for death.

CHAPTER FIVE

Laughing with the pleasure of a hard ride and the best mount, Sunkawakan Iyopeya crested the rise above his Cheyenne brothers' village well before the rest of the hunting party. There would be no more jesting about who had the superior mounts. He captured and broke the best horses the Plains had to offer. No one would dispute it now.

The sun was at its highest, and the heat lay on the land like a smoldering buffalo hide. He wiped sweat from his brow and surveyed the village. Few people were about, a few children playing in the dust at the opposite end of the village and two captives, one minding her cooking fire, the other sitting. Reined in by his master's hands, Sunkawakan Iyopeya's mount blew out an impatient breath and pawed the earth. The hunting party was right behind them. Jubilant with their catch, the men rode hard to the rise.

Mindful of the women and children, he turned and shouted, "Halt."

They didn't heed his warning but flew past him riding straight into the heart of the village. This was not part of the agreement. They knew children and the elderly wandered between the teepees. But Sunkawakan Iyopeya knew their pride was at stake. They couldn't be bested by a Lakota Sioux.

Leaning over his mount, he spurred his horse to greater speed, hoping to beat the men to the village.

"Hiyah," he shouted to his stallion. His heart banged in his chest like a ceremonial drum.

He'd passed all but two of the horsemen by the time they reached the center of the camp. He could see only one of the women, fear and defiance playing across her features. The first horseman managed to avoid riding over her. The second couldn't stop and plowed into her, knocking her to the ground. Sunkawakan Iyopeya could hear the rest of the hunting party, twelve men, hard on his horse's hooves.

She'd gotten to her hands and knees, trying to rise again. Leaping from his mount's back, he fell onto the woman, sheltering her thin body with his own and rolling them between the hooves of the oncoming horses. One hoof caught him a glancing blow, but he didn't loosen his grip.

They rolled into a teepee, bringing down the whole thing.

Her breath blew hot and choppy on his neck. She smelled of corn and woman musk. For a brief moment, he cradled her in his arms.

"Get off me, you heathen," her muffled voice said from beneath him.

The last stretch had been a race for her life, and it had left him winded as though he'd been in battle. When she pushed at his shoulders, he realized his full weight pressed her into the ground.

He raised his head and stared down at the bundle in his arms. Her face was different than any he had ever seen. Her skin, the parts not covered in soot, was brown like the nuts that fell in the forest. Her eyes were like honey, and they spat fire.

Rolling off and standing in almost one motion, he reached down for her. She slapped his hand away and struggled to her feet.

"Good with the horses not with the women," one of the men from the hunting party shouted. The other Cheyenne laughed.

If the words eased their wounded pride, he'd let them have the last say. He needed their good will. He hoped when the time came they would band together with the Lakota to drive the white man from their land.

Hands on her slim hips, the brown-skinned woman glared at him and the other men. Tall and straight-boned, even with a torn and stained gown, she held herself with pride. The focus of her anger appeared to be him, even though he'd been the one to save her. He'd never understand women.

An angry old woman burrowed from beneath the ruins of the teepee. She teetered on bowed legs and stared with confusion at the people who surrounded her shelter.

"Forgive us, old mother," Sunkawakan Iyopeya said. "We will build you another teepee."

"Speak for yourself," one of the hunters shouted. "*You* destroyed her hut." The others laughed.

The old one's mouth twisted in a snarl. She turned away and started to search among the ruins of her home.

Sunkawakan Iyopeya faced the men. "You did not heed my command to halt."

"You meant to best us. We knew your intent."

The men laughed. The laughter turned to shouts and hoots as the men pointed behind him. Sunkawakan Iyopeya turned. The old one was beating the brown woman.

Before he thought about the wisdom of his actions, he snatched the whip from the old woman. She turned her displeasure on him, kicking and screaming hate words in the Cheyenne language.

Hopping off his horse, To'too'he grabbed the old woman's hands. "Cease, you shame me in front of our blood brother." The old woman spat at To'too'he's feet and lumbered away.

To Sunkawakan Iyopeya he said, "She's just a slave." He jerked his chin in the direction of the brown woman. "I traded a new bow for her. The Comanche were happy to be rid of that one. They said the evil spirits followed her."

Sunkawakan Iyopeya studied the captive. Her gaze narrowed on To'too'he, and her nose flared as though she smelled the stench of a rotting buffalo carcass. Sunkawakan Iyopeya suppressed a smile. His Cheyenne brother did smell.

When her gaze traveled to him, her brow creased, and she tilted her head. What was she thinking? Did she wonder if he was a good man? An honorable man? For the first time in many snows, he wanted a woman to think him worthy. He wanted *this* woman to find him worthy.

The yapping of dogs and the shouts of the young and elderly as they left the safety of their teepees broke the spell. The brown one picked up the poles and began to rebuild the old woman's teepee.

He had been invited by To'too'he to share his shelter and food. Would the old lady suffer him in her tent now that he had saved the young captive from her anger?

He dropped the reins of his horse and picked up one of the poles. At first the honey-eyed woman glared at him with suspicion. Then with a shrug, she continued with her task. Her movements were like the gentle sway of the trees on a warm summer day. Her curly hair fluttered against her skin. The women of his tribe had long black hair that fell straight as a cradleboard against their back. The woman's hair was alive, springy and tangled like river moss. His fingers twitched, wanting to reach out and pull on a stray curl. From the looks she'd cast in his direction, she would not welcome his touch. He would have to work hard to change her feelings. He reached for the buffalo skin and helped her stretched it around the staked poles.

To'too'he was a good warrior and respected by the young men of his tribe. But Sunkawakan Iyopeya did not like him. The Cheyenne was without honor. He mistreated his horses and did not respect the women in his life.

Sunkawakan Iyopeya was conflicted. If he accepted the Cheyenne's hospitality, he could spend a few days in the company of a man he did not respect, but he would also be close to the brown one. He glanced at her from the corner of his eyes. She had caught her bottom lip between her teeth as she fought to wrap the buffalo skins around one of the poles.

He took a deep breath and gathered his wits. He had a mission: find out whom among the Cheyenne would stand with the Sioux.

The wasi'chu would soon drive all the Plains Indians into one small area. He'd seen this in a vision during his Sun Dance ceremony many winters ago. He did not believe in those pieces of paper they called treaties. Those markings on paper could be easily forgotten when it suited the white man's purpose. He would travel to the fort to hear the falsehoods that would fall from the white man's mouth—to judge for himself.

He would accept To'too'he's shelter, but only so he could persuade the warrior of the need to band together with the Sioux.

Because soon there would be war.

The wind blew embers up from the cooking fires. Julia batted away the sparks that landed on her only dress. It would rain tonight. Not a gentle rain but a thundering that would rock the ground beneath the teepee.

She turned her face up to the gathering night. Felt the caress of the wind. Mama had said the wind brought change. What changes would be in store for her? So far, they'd not been good ones. She'd also grown lazy—forgetting her purpose. Freedom. Canada. Winter would be here soon and she needed to be away from these Indians.

She didn't look up when someone squatted by her fire and extended a wooden bowl. She placed sliced meat in the eating dish. When the person didn't move away, she raised her eyes. Her heart fluttered in her chest like a bird trying to break free from its cage. It was the one from earlier in

the day. The one who'd fallen on her and rolled them into
the old woman's teepee. The one who'd saved her.

With a bold gaze, he watched her with eyes as black as
the coming night. He pointed at his chest and spoke words
she didn't understand. He then pointed a finger at her. Was
he asking her name? Had the words he'd spoken been his
name?

"Julia."

He frowned and let the word fall from his lips. It came
out sounding like "oolea" She couldn't fault him, it was
better than his name sounded to her. She would call him
Horseman since many horses in the camp belonged to him.

Someone shoved her. Only the fast hands of the
Horseman, reaching across the flames, kept her from falling
into the fire. Greasy Hair stood above her, a scowl on his
ugly face. He pointed to the men around the fire and then at
the roasting venison. She set about slicing hunks of meat
from the roast.

He'd meant to shame her, but he'd brought her back to
her God given senses.

She shouldn't be making cow eyes at Horseman. He was
a man like all the rest. And she didn't need a man in her
life. She was headed north. When she could make her
letters and read better, she'd open a school and teach all the
escaped slaves so they could have better lives.

But first she needed warmer clothes for her journey
because the nights were growing cooler. Most importantly,
she needed to find out how to get to Canada.

Energy surrounded the newcomer as he spoke excitedly
to the younger men. Would he help her? As though feeling
her gaze, his eyes sought hers across the campfire.

The whispers of the wind and the voices of the people
fell away. It was if he tried to speak to her with his eyes.
She leaned forward to catch his silent words. Someone said
something to him and only then did he turn away. Night
sounds returned. Laughter bounced around the circle of

villagers. Air left her body in a rush. She'd been holding her breath.

She jumped up and stumbled over feet in her haste to pick up bits of wood, buffalo chips, anything to keep the fire going. Anything to take her mind off what had just happened. Anything to not think about this Horseman.

Later, when the last of the meat was carved and stored, Julia sought her sleeping pallet. As the night filled with the sound of thunder and the sky lit as bright as day, she was grateful for her space inside the stale teepee. As the first drops of rain hit the buffalo skins, she settled deeper into her bed. Across the space, the old woman snored.

Greasy Hair and some of the other men, including the Horseman, had been in deep discussion around the dying fires. She was grateful for the peace, but she wondered what they talked about. They didn't speak of crops since she hadn't seen any growing. Did they speak of the number of scalps they'd taken? She shivered, wanting to hold on to hers long enough to escape.

Her peace didn't last long. The flap over the teepee opened and fresh rain air and a loud voice filled the space.

Julia squeezed her eyes shut, but not before she saw a tall, broad shouldered figure entered behind Greasy Hair.

Horseman.

Pretending sleep, she watched the two men through half closed lids. Greasy Hair pointed to a place near his mother. Horseman, with a blanket draped over his arm settled down for the night. She froze, barely breathing as Greasy Hair studied her pallet.

After a long moment, he took to his sleeping mat near the back of the teepee. She relaxed. Maybe having his friend here would keep the old woman's son on his side of the tent.

Horseman rubbed her bare thigh. He smelled...

She jerked awake.

Greasy Hair knelt at the foot of her sleeping mat, his dirty paw stroking her thigh. He placed his finger to his lips, silencing her.

She kicked out, catching him in the chest.

He fell, landing on his ass. Moving as quickly as a jackrabbit, he covered her body with his, pinning her legs.

She screamed.

Sunkawakan Iyopeya sprang to his feet, reaching for his bow.

By the glow of the fire's embers, two bodies wriggled on the pallet in the far corner.

To'too'he mated with the brown-skinned woman. The woman who had watched Sunkawakan Iyopeya over the campfire. His disappointment almost strangled him.

He frowned. Her sounds did not seem as though To'too'he pleasured her. The noise that brought him out of slumber came back to him.

In two strides, he was beside the pallet and had To'too'he by the neck, yanking him off the woman.

The captive scrambled to her knees, covering her body with her torn clothes.

Keeping his voice low to avoid waking the old woman, Sunkawakan Iyopeya whispered, "Do not dishonor yourself by forcing an unwilling woman."

To'too'he's eyes blazed in the dim light. "She is mine."

Sunkawakan Iyopeya took a deep breath, trying to calm his racing heart and rid himself of his anger. It would not do to let his Cheyenne brother know that he too desired the woman. "There are many women in the village who would be honored to lie with you. Why force yourself on one who does not want you?"

To'too'he jerked from Sunkawakan Iyopeya's hold and stomped out of the teepee.

The silence in the hut was filled with the snores of the old mother and the ragged breathing of the woman.

He moved toward her.

She scrambled out of reach. Like a cougar's, her golden eyes blazed fire, not fear.

He backed slowly away. Grabbing his blanket, he left the teepee.

After checking on his horses, he spread his blanket in a dry spot under some pines. He would not sleep tonight, but the fresh air would clear his mind.

Had he made an enemy of To'too'he by coming to the woman's aid? Was one woman worth losing the support of this Cheyenne tribe? He thought not.

At dawn he would leave.

CHAPTER SIX

A few sunsets later on a rise across the river from Fort Laramie, Sunkawakan Iyopeya sat astride his horse and watched the Whites scurry around the grounds like ants.

His horse shifted restlessly beneath him. White streams of hot air blew from the stallion's nose and disappeared into the cool morning air.

He patted the animal's sides. "All is well, boy." But all was not well. He had failed. Failed to make the tribes see the danger.

Hundreds of his brothers would gather in a few days to sign the paper the white man called a treaty. A treaty that would allow whites to move further into Indian land, killing the buffalo and ravaging the ground the Sioux, Cheyenne, and Arapahoe had called home for many winters.

Red Cloud had believed him. But the two of them were no match for the trinkets the white man brought as gifts. His gaze moved from mountains to the open land. Soon this would disappear. Would his children's children see the land as he did now? He thought not. He turned his horse away from the Fort and headed toward his village.

Julia rose from her pallet and stepped outside. The air was sharp with the lateness of the year. Frost covered the ground and her breath flowed from her mouth in white puffs. She hurried to the river. There she kept an eye on the thicket of trees that surrounded the water as she completed her morning ritual. She didn't want to be caught unaware by the animals that roamed the area—both the four and two footed ones. Two good things had come from the night the Horseman had pulled Greasy Hair off her. She could move about the camp freely during the day, and the old woman had put Greasy Hair out of her teepee. He now lived in the unmarried men's shelter.

When Julia arrived back in the camp, the old woman was moving around inside the teepee. Julia built a fire and stirred together ground corn and water. She baked the paste on a flat clay stone until golden brown. The old woman liked this hoecake for her morning meal. Although Greasy Hair's mother still treated Julia poorly, the hatred had turned from black to gray. Maybe it was the hoecakes.

Raised voices in the next teepee drew Julia's attention away from the cooking fire.

"What ails the captive?" she asked Greasy Hair's mother when the old woman limped out of the teepee. Over the last several months Julia had learned a little of the language and now knew the white woman was sick. She was surprised the red-haired woman had lasted this long.

Greasy Hair's mother lowered her tiny body to the ground next to the fire. She greedily reached for the hoecake. "She has the ague. Her body burns."

The old woman ate and then wiped her hands on her already dirty skirt before packing her pipe with tobacco.

Keeping one eye on her fires and roasting meat, Julia watched all morning the comings and goings from the next teepee. The women went about their daily chores as if there was not a sick person in their hut. "Is no one caring for her?" Julia finally asked the old woman.

"If she is meant to live, she'll live," the old woman said flatly. She lowered her blanket from around her head as the morning sun warmed her shoulders.

Just as she knew they'd let her die if she were ill, Julia knew the white woman would die in the next few days without care.

Julia's mother had been the healer in the quarter. She'd taught Julia a few things about healing—like the flowers and leaves that grew down by this river could be used for fever.

When the old woman took her midday sleep, Julia would collect the leaves. As she waited, her mind filled with images of the white woman in the few months since she'd come to the camp. Her eyes often sought Julia's with awareness. But the woman never said a word. Once or twice as she sat in the sun outside her tent, she had rocked and crooned to an imaginary babe in her arms. The Indians had walked a wide path around her. Why hadn't they killed her? They had such cruelty within them.

Finally Greasy Hair's mother rose on unsteady legs and wobbled into the tent. When the sound of snoring drifted out of the teepee, Julia pulled the meat from the fire. In case someone asked where she headed, she grabbed a water bucket and hurried toward the river.

The days grew shorter now. The sun had started to sink behind the hills before she found enough of the tall stalks and white flowers that had been plentiful during the summer months. She had to hurry and return before the old woman woke.

After ripping a few of the plants from the soil, she was almost back to camp when she remembered she'd left the bucket by the river.

She spun around and stopped.

Greasy Hair stepped into her path. Grinning, exposing brown stubby teeth, he slunk toward her like a barnyard cat stalking a chicken.

Her mouth went dry. Could she outrun him?

She moved backwards and slipped on the muddy path. When she went down, he was on her.

She tried to squirm away, but her legs were pinned beneath his weight, making her attempts to inch up the path, useless.

Please. Please. She didn't know who she prayed to. God had deserted her a long time ago. One hand pushed him away, the other searched for something, anything to use as a weapon. Sticks, dried leaves and pebbles passed through her fingers.

His man thing lay on her thigh like a cold worm.

Her fingers touched something rough and hard.

A rock.

A *large* rock.

She couldn't close her hand around it, but she gripped as much of it as she could between her fingers. Before she could lose her courage, she brought the rock down hard on top of his head. He stared up at her in confusion, grunted, and then ripped her shift. She hit him again. The force of the blow made her arm tremble. He clutched his head and moaned. She raised her hand to strike him a third time, but the sight of blood running over his fingers and down his face made her stomach twist and heave. Pushing him completely off her body, she scooted from beneath him.

Her legs shook. Greasy Hair's hand reached out blindly for her.

"Maim him," the voice in her head said. "Crush his fingers." Crush the fingers that wanted to pinch and twist the only thing she could call her own—her body.

The weight of her misery almost choked her. As she stared down at the bleeding man, the world around her continued as though nothing had happened. Birds called to one another, the water rippled to the rocky shore, the orange and brown leaves showing the first hint of the coming winter rustled over her head.

Her breath caught in her throat. Where did she go? Where did she hide? There was nowhere to run. Nowhere to hide. Not now. Later in the spring if they let her live after what she'd done to Greasy Hair, she would run.

Kneeling, she picked up the now wilted plants and walked wobbly kneed toward the river. She filled the bucket with water before washing the roots of the plant.

When she turned to head back up the path to the camp, Greasy Hair was gone.

The white woman died.

Julia's arms trembled as she dug a hole for the body. She'd taken it upon herself to give the woman a Christian burial. The Indians had just wrapped her body and left her outside the tent. Left her for Julia to find the next morning.

The previous evening, she'd brewed the leaves of the plant into a tea. When the old woman had gone visiting and the neighboring women went to the river, Julia had snuck into the teepee.

The white woman lay on her pallet, her face as pale as a new moon. At first Julia thought she was dead, but then the woman meowed like a newborn kitten. Julia had tried to get her to drink the tea, but the brown liquid had dribbled from her mouth and very little reached her belly. The Indian women had returned from their chores and chased Julia out of the teepee.

She had to hurry. The sun set much earlier as the days grew shorter. She needed to dig this hole before it became too dark to see. She also needed a deep hole so animals wouldn't unearth the body.

Her palms burned and her shoulders ached from clenching the wooden stick.

A twig snapped.

Her head jerked up. Heart hammering in her chest, she gripped the stick like a weapon, prepared to fight off Greasy Hair.

She blinked. Not believing what she saw.

Horseman stood on the other side of the shallow grave.

What was he doing here?

He didn't say a word but reached for the stick.

She stepped back, clutching the wood to her chest. Why did he want it?

His gaze traveled over her face, her body. She swiped at a strand of hair and wrapped it around her ear. His gaze followed the motion. Suddenly she was conscious of her sweaty unwashed body. Her face heated in shame. She hated this place, hated she'd ended up still enslaved, hated this man saw her at her worst.

His dark eyes held hers as he reached out slowly. This time she didn't resist when his fingers closed around the handle.

Surely he didn't mean to help. Why now? None of his kind helped the white woman when she was alive. This wasn't his village, but weren't they all alike? Hating the white man? Hating her? She didn't ask to be here. This woman, now dead and ready to make her transition, didn't ask to be dragged from her home. So why did he want to help now the white woman was dead?

Exhausted, Julia retreated and sank onto her haunches beside the swaddled body. Horseman removed his buckskin shirt.

The Indians had been almost naked from the moment she'd encountered them. But there was something about this man being clothed one minute and shirtless the next that made her swallow hard against a dry throat.

She glanced hurriedly away, but the image of his lean, corded body was branded on her brain.

He worked quickly using a shovel-like stick he'd brought and in no time had a hole deep and wide enough to place the white woman in. Daylight fading, he picked up the shrouded form and placed it in the ground. Then he began shoving the dirt on top of the body.

Something needed to be said over the woman's grave. Bo had always been the one to say a prayer over the departed back on the plantation. But Bo wasn't here.

Could she say the right words? It didn't matter. She was the only one who could. She only hoped when her time came someone would say words over her.

When she touched his arm, the muscles underneath his buckskin shirt bunched. He stopped, his black eyes searching hers. If only they could talk to each other. How could she tell him what she wanted to do?

She pressed her hands together, indicating prayer. He stared blankly at her.

Sighing, she stepped up to the hole until her bare feet were inches from the opening. He sprang forward, grabbing her around the waist. She would have laughed if the occasion hadn't been so sad.

Did he think she wanted to kill herself? Not that she hadn't thought about in the months since she'd run from the Donnelly plantation.

She struggled out of his hold and pushed him away. Holding her hands again, she bowed her head. "Dear Lord, receive this woman into your care. Reunite her with her family…"

Julia searched for more to say, but the words caught in her throat. She felt more alone at this moment than any time since she'd run. When she died there'd be no one to mourn her. Tears fell on her chapped hands. She glanced sideways at Horseman, and when she saw that he stared at the hole and not her, she swiped at her face.

"Amen."

She fell to her knees and started to push the earth back into the hole. The dirt hit the body with a thud, and for a moment, Julia couldn't bring herself to fill the grave. If the white woman had any family left, they'd never know where she was buried. Never know what had become of her. But none of Julia's family would know what had become of her. They probably thought she was dead. She wouldn't think about that now. If she did, she'd crawl in the hole with the poor, mute woman.

Horseman, who had respected her silence, began to refill the hole. She helped him. When they finished, he gathered stones to pile on top of the grave.

She gave the burial site one last glance before following him up the trail towards the camp.

His scent of horse and male sweat carried on the wind. Before he topped the rise, she caught up with him and touched his arm. He turned, a question in his eyes. Hastily, she dropped her hand, twisting it in the cloth of her dress.

She didn't know if he would understand her, but she said, "Thank you."

He nodded once and continued on ahead of her to the camp.

When they reached the old woman's teepee, Julia stopped in surprise. A haunch of some meat roasted over a fire she hadn't built. The old woman sat grinding corn and didn't glance up when they approached. When Julia tried to take the pestle and bowl from her, the old crone almost hissed.

"Sit." Horseman took her arm and pointed to an area on the opposite side of the fire from Greasy Hair's mother. Julia didn't know what surprised her more—that he'd spoken a word she understood—or she wasn't beaten for not being here to start the evening meal.

Horseman knelt in front of the old woman. He spoke to her, using his hands and some words of the woman's language. She spat her reply. Horseman glanced over at Julia. Without another word, he stalked over to the next teepee where the women watched his approach with wide frightened eyes.

He spoke to them once again using his hands. One of the women disappeared inside her shelter. When she returned, she carried a deerskin dress and a pair of deerskin boots with leggings. Horseman returned to the fire and handed the items to Julia. She accepted them in stunned silence.

"Tomorrow," he commanded.

Tomorrow? Tomorrow what?

He stalked out of the camp before she could ask him what was so all-fired important about tomorrow.

A hint of gray mixed with the blackness of the sky as Julia made her way to the river. Frost dusted the path. Rarely had it gotten cold enough in Louisiana for ice to coat the grass. Now the ice crunched under Julia's bare feet, her toes curling against the coldness. She washed quickly, her skin pricking in the cold morning air. She dressed with haste in her new finery. Even though the clothes had been worn by another, she was as proud of them as though they'd been made especially for her.

Why had the Horseman given her the clothes? Did he pity her? It didn't matter. She needed the dress and foot covering—especially when she ran. The snow would be upon the land soon, and she didn't know how long she could live among the Cheyenne. Greasy Hair would eventually try again to stake his claim to her, and she would have to kill him.

When she returned to camp Horseman sat on a large black horse outside the old woman's teepee. He held the reins of a small pony.

Julia put distance between herself, the horses and the man. Squatting, she started the morning fire.

"Aieee…"

Startled, Julia turned but not quick enough. The old woman rushed at her like the wind during a violent storm. She shoved Julia, shaking her fist at her and pointing at Horseman.

Julia picked herself up and brushed away the rocks that had bitten into her arm. What was wrong with the old she-devil? Was she angry because Julia hadn't started the morning meal?

Horseman said something sharp to the old woman. She scuttled back into her teepee.

"Come," he said, holding the reins of the smaller horse out to Julia.

Rising, she glanced from him to the horse and back. *Come where?*

But then all the pieces finally came together. The warmer clothes, the respect the old one had shown Horseman and now him here with a horse for her. She'd been traded off again. This time to this—this *horse man.*

"Come," he said again, moving the pony closer to her.

She backed away. Leaving this camp had been the only thing on her mind since she arrived. But she wanted to leave on her own terms—by herself, not with another capturer. Her knees threatened to buckle.

Why did he want her? A chill colder than the one she'd felt while washing at the river ran through her body. Did he want the same thing from her that Greasy Hair had? *Of course he does.* Men only wanted to rut on a woman, fill her belly with child, and move on to the next female.

"Come." This time the command rang with authority. He leapt off his horse, grasped her around the waist and hoisted her onto the pony. She sat on the beast in stunned rage. Why hadn't she run when Greasy Hair had tried to lay with her?

The old woman watched them from the opening of her teepee. As much as the old woman disliked her, she wouldn't just give away a slave. Horseman had paid the old woman. Since Julia had never seen the Indians deal in coin, she knew horses must have changed hands.

Horseman was a different breed of man. Shrewd, watchful, and smart. He'd studied her over the flames when she'd first met him. He'd taken her measure. If he wanted her body, he wouldn't be put off as easily as Greasy Hair had been. Running from him wouldn't be easy.

Julia took a deep breath, pushed down her desperation and turned the pony to follow the Horseman. She'd bide her time. When the right moment came, she'd run. She'd be slave to no man.

CHAPTER SEVEN

Sunkawakan Iyopeya judged there was an hour of sun left. The days had grown shorter as winter approached. Would he make it back to his camp before the first snows? If he traveled alone, he wouldn't care. He often wintered on the land, setting snares for food, traveling in drifts up to his horses' forelocks. But he wasn't alone. He glanced back at the woman. Crippled old women rode a horse better than this brown woman. She'd fallen off the pony more times than he cared to count. A journey that should have taken to the new moon would now take twice that long—if the snows didn't blow sooner from the north.

He scanned the horizon. Except for an outcropping of boulders in the distance, the land lay flat and barren as far as the eye could see. The rocks would provide very little protection against the wind, but searching for a better campsite with darkness approaching would be too risky with a green rider. He spurred the horses on.

Later, he rubbed down the horses and fed them. The woman picked up buffalo chips and groaned with every step she took.

The wind whipped the grasses and howled across the flat land as he and the woman ate in silence around the flickering flames. She moved closer and closer to the fire as she chewed slowly on the dried meat and berries. He rose and removed a blanket from the roll and placed it around her shoulders.

"Thank you." Her voice was barely a whisper above the wind.

How had such a woman come to travel without the protection of a tribe? From To'too'he, Sunkawakan Iyopeya had learned the Comanche found her wandering in the lands just west of the Great River.

Was her man dead? Was that why she traveled alone?

She drew the blanket tighter around her small body but could not seem to still the tremors that shook her.

He rose. Taking another blanket from the roll, he stretched out on the cold earth close to the fire. Without dung to keep the fire burning through the night, she would freeze.

"Come," he said, patting the ground next to him. The warmth from both their bodies would make the night bearable.

She stared at him, her eyes large like a frightened doe. She jerked her head around and stared mulishly into the flames while she continued to tremble.

Stubborn woman. He rolled into his blanket and closed his eyes.

Sometime in the night, he felt her ease down near him. Later as the dawn drifted closer, her body relaxed and curled around his back.

Julia woke to a gentle touch on her shoulder and frost covering the ground. The sun had
just crested the horizon, and the horses were ready for travel. Horseman handed her more of the dried meat. She was beginning to hate the sight and smell of deer meat. She ate slowly as she thought about the previous night.

It had been colder than she'd imagined. She'd sat by the fire until the embers barely glowed and then stretched out with her blanket. The wind whipped around her head, through the blanket and around her feet. No amount of tugging, crunching and huddling made her warm enough to sleep. Not a sound came from Horseman on the other side of the almost dead fire. How could he sleep so soundly? Keeping her hands inside the blanket and her chin tucked, she vowed to make it to morning.

The restless motion of the horses woke her. She sat straight up, blanket forgotten, as she strained to see in the blackness. Had something moved out there? Shadows shifted and she swore something four-footed crouched just beyond their small camp.

"Horseman," she hissed. She'd never called him by name and definitely never uttered the name she given him. Now, she was past caring if she offended him. When he didn't respond, she crawled around the banked fire to his side, rocks biting into her hands and knees.

"Horseman," she whispered. "Coyotes." Was her imagination playing tricks on her?

When he didn't answer, she thought about going back to her side of the fire and trying to sleep. She didn't move.

She sat cross-legged next to him, her blanket tucked around her, her hair whipping around her face in the wind. Scanning the darkness, it was impossible to distinguish the sky from the land. It all blended together.

Her body jerked. She'd fallen asleep sitting up. Morning would come and she'd tumble off her pony. She needed rest. What would it hurt to lie here next to him? He wouldn't know. She would wake and be on her side of the fire before he stirred.

Now as she broke her fast, she realized he'd let her sleep longer than usual. Had he really been asleep when she'd crept over to his side of the fire? Had he known she'd been up hours, trembling and staring into the darkness, waiting for wild animals to attack? She gritted her teeth with the shame of it. She wasn't some fragile woman who was afraid of her shadow.

I got courage.

Jumping up she rolled up her blanket and marched off to the other side of the boulders to do her business. When she

returned to her pony she ignored Horseman's cupped hands
and flung herself on the back of the pony. With as much
dignity as she could manage, she maneuvered her body into
an upright position, ready for the day's ride.

The land had changed in the last day or two. Mountains
appeared in the distance, their tips coated with snow.

Julia huddled in her blanket with the cold wind making
her eyes sting and her nose run. She and Horseman sat on
their mounts across the river from many buildings and
many white folks who scurried around covered wagons.

She watched him from the corner of her eye. *Please
don't go down there.*

She and the Indian had only communicated with hand
signals and a few white people words. How could she tell
him she was a runaway and people might be looking for
her? Mistress Donnelly did not forget about her property.
She didn't walk away from money, and Julia was money.

When Horseman spurred his horse across the river, Julia
groaned but kneed her pony to follow. Freezing water
splashed on her legs, soaking through her dress, making her
shiver more. The sun's weak rays were no match for the
stiff cold wind blowing down off the mountains.

She pulled her blanket up over her hair so only her face
was visible. She kept her eyes downcast as they trotted on
the path between white washed buildings. This was the first
time she'd been among whites since she fled the plantation.
She expected at any moment for someone to grab the reins
of her horse and shout "runaway" and pull her from the
back of her mount.

But instead of shouts, there was silence. The silence
made Julia more uneasy than whispers would have. When
Horseman's mount trotted past, one wide-eyed woman
wearing blue calico with frizzy brown hair escaping from
her matching bonnet pushed her child behind her skirts.
The child, a boy, quickly peered around his mother's body

to stare with big eyes after the Indian. A man, the woman's husband Julia guessed, placed a hand on the woman's arm, before lifting his rifle to his shoulder. Julia put her knees to her pony's stomach to catch up with Horseman.

He stopped in front of a building that looked like all the others, white-washed boards with a balcony running along the second level.

"Would ya look at that?"

Two men leaned over the railing. Dressed only in pants and shirts, their suspenders fell alongside their hips. Their shirts, maybe once white, were stained brown in spots.

"It's an Injun and his nigger squaw."

Julia could feel the heat rise in her face. The words stung. Not that she hadn't been called a *nigger* before, but this far away from the plantation she thought things would be different. She thought a lot of things would be different.

It was a good thing Horseman didn't understand them, though from the straightening of his shoulders, he understood the tones of the men's voices. He tied his mount to a hitching post and signaled for her to get down. She slid off her pony, and he caught her around the waist, easing her to the ground. His hands were warm and firm around her body. Making herself as small as possible, she followed him into the building.

A wall of noise hit her when she stepped into the hot room. Men's voices. *White* men's voices. She pulled her blanket tighter around her face and kept her eyes downcast.

Did they know she was a runaway? Probably didn't matter. They'd sell her if they could.

She forced her breathing to slow. *I ain't afraid. I ain't afraid.* Breathe in. Breathe out. She gagged.

In the last few months, she'd been among unwashed bodies, dead bodies and rotting fish in the bayou, but nothing prepared her for the stench that filled this large room. She lifted her gaze just enough to study the room.

With flesh still attached, animal skins of different colors and thickness lay piled atop a long wooden table.

Surrounding the table were twenty or thirty men whose voices had fallen silent one by one as they became aware of her and Horseman.

Rather than look anyone in the eye, she studied the dirty tobacco stained floors.

"Whatcha want in here?"

She glanced up quickly.

The voice belonged to a short man with a drooping mustache. Wearing a blacksmith's apron, he stood behind the table. Guns of different sizes were spread out on the counter. He stroked one with a long crooked finger.

"Fitzpatrick," Horseman said.

Julia stared at the Indian. How many times had he said the name to get it to sound so good, so right?

"He means old Thomas," another man said, "the Injun agent." This one spoke around a plug of chewing tobacco lodged in his cheek.

"He ain't here," the man behind the counter said. When his gaze shifted Julia's way, she dropped her head and stared at the floor again.

"And won't ever be here for the likes of you," someone in the crowd shouted. Were they talking to her or Horseman?

A mumble of agreement filled the room.

The space seemed to shrink, and Julia had to force down the urge to back toward the door. While her heart hammered in her ears, Horseman seemed unaffected. But she saw his hands clench and then slowly open.

What had possessed him to come here? They should have travelled directly to his village. Now they were both going to be strung up.

Staring at the men's knees, she saw them shift almost as one, advancing toward her and Horseman.

The creak of the door and a blast of cold air made them hesitate.

"Good morning and a fine one it is."

For one moment, Julia thought she was back at the plantation and Master Donnelly was still alive. She turned slowly.

A priest stood in the door, black frock and all. For the first time in her life, Julia was happy to see a Catholic man of God. She was very familiar with priests. Both Master and Mistress Donnelly had been Catholic. When the Master had been on his deathbed, Father Gronin lived at the plantation, ready to give the Master the last rites and save as many of the *heathen blacks* as he could.

"What do we have here?" the priest asked as he walked toward Horseman. Julia waited, her breath locked in her lungs.

"He's looking for Thomas Fitzpatrick, Father Keegan," black apron said.

"Ah," the priest nodded and for the first time noticed Julia. "You are with him?"

Julia opened her mouth but no words came out. She nodded.

"Do you speak his language?" the priest asked.

She shook her head.

"Hmm..." The priest rubbed his chin as he inspected them.

Julia's stomach growled.

Dropping his hands, the priest smiled, a gesture that didn't ease Julia's discomfort. The overseer had smiled before the whip came down on one of the slaves' back.

"How about some breakfast?" Father Keegan asked.

As much as her mouth watered at the thought of something other than dried deer meat and berries, her gut said *run*. But she was also aware of the wall of white men that surrounded her and Horseman. If they went with the priest, it might get them out of this room alive. Dealing with one white man was easier than dealing with twenty.

"Thank you, sir," she said in her best Mistress Donnelly's voice. *Fool. Hope you not jumping from the kettle into the fire.*

The white-haired priest gestured toward the door. This time Julia was in front of Horseman leaving the room.

They followed the priest outside and across the muddy path to a building that looked the same as the one they'd left. He took them through one of the many doors into a parlor with two rocking chairs placed around a roaring fireplace.

Even though the heat from the fire drew her, Julia didn't step far into the room. Horseman stepped around her and moved to a small table with pictures arranged neatly on its surface.

"Mrs. Gershon," the priest shouted.

A plump woman with brown hair streaked with gray poked her head into the room. She stared openmouthed at Julia and Horseman.

"Some breakfast, if you *please*."

Mrs. Gershon's mouth snapped shut. Throwing a last glance at them, she backed out of the door.

The priest's attention moved from Julia to Horseman. "How have you been, Sunkawakan Iyopeya?"

Julia frowned. *Sunka...Sunka...* Horseman had said something similar two moons ago over the campfire back in Greasy Hair's village. This must be his Indian name.

"I survive, but my people are hungry."

Julia blinked once, twice. Heat flooded her face and her eyes almost crossed with anger as she thought about the long days and nights of silence. He spoke like a white man.

Her gaze flew to the priest's face. And this one wasn't surprised. The old man knew the Indian and knew he could speak. What had they been playing at over at the fur place?

Father Keegan's gaze flickered to Julia. "This is your woman?"

"Yes."

What! She was not his woman. She opened her mouth to tell the priest that very thing but clamped her lips together. What was she to him? She wasn't his captive? He hadn't tied her hands or feet. She roamed the campgrounds at night as freely as he did. When they slept, she wasn't bound. If she said she wasn't his woman, would he start treating her like a captive?

Julia clenched her hands in the deerskin dress so tight she felt pain in her knuckles. She wasn't anyone's woman. She was free. Head bowed to hide the anger, she struggled with the words that wanted to burst from her mouth. Words that would make Horseman tie her up. Words that would take away what little freedom she had with him. Maybe as long as he believed she wanted to be his woman, the longer he'd let her move around freely. The easier it would be to flee.

So caught up in her own thoughts, she'd missed the conversation between the priest and Sunk...Sunk... Horseman.

"I don't know where the wagons are," the priest said.

Horseman narrowed his eyes.

"I have no reason to lie," the priest said, his words low and soft. He held Horseman's gaze.

The Indian nodded slowly. "But your word will not feed my people. We do not want your scraps. We need provisions to get us to the spring thaw, then the buffalo will be plentiful, and we can trade for other supplies."

Mrs. Gershon entered with a tray of food that gave off a heavenly aroma—bacon, bread. Julia inhaled deeply.

"Go back to your village. When the wagons come, I will personally bring the provisions to you."

Horseman's mouth tightened, his eyes flashing like black lightning. "What about food for the Cheyenne and the Shoshone? They also signed the white man's treaty.

"Maybe we should take the provisions being loaded in those wagons." Horseman pointed toward the fort's grounds. "Or take the sacks of grain from those who travel across our land, killing the buffalo."

The priest's blue eyes widened with alarm. "Think before you act. Innocent people will die."

"Yes," Horseman said. "Many people, both whites and Indians, will die."

The priest turned his pleading gaze on Julia.

What could she do? Her thoughts meant nothing to this Indian. He hadn't graced her with one sentence in the weeks they'd traveled together. He'd shared more of his thoughts and feelings with his horses than with her.

Horseman picked up a frame from the small table by the window, studying it. It held an image of a small yellow-haired boy of six or seven years. "Many Sioux children have already died. Have you thought about that, black coat? Take heed, the time will come when the Indian will no longer peacefully smoke their pipes and allow you to take food from their children's mouths. They will strike." He slammed the picture face down on the table. The crack of splintering glass filled the silence. He turned on his heel and stalked out of the priest's quarters.

Julia didn't know what surprised her more—that he spoke so good or that there was so much fire in his words.

"He will be killed." The old man looked smaller, older, and his long coat hung like a sack on his bony body.

At the emotion in his voice, Julia's heart twisted in her chest like clothes being hung out for drying. She couldn't meet the old man's gaze. She didn't want to see the sadness that made his eyes dark holes in a moon white face. She didn't want to feel anything for Horseman. His death meant nothing to her. If he died, she'd be free.

"Give him wise counsel," Father Keegan said, "or he and his kind will be slaughtered like sheep."

Julia opened her mouth to tell the priest Horseman had lied. She wasn't his woman and held no sway over his actions. She just wanted her freedom.

The smell of the food now made a taste like sour mash rise in her throat. She hastened toward the door, leaving behind the warmth, the fresh-cooked food and the sound of doom echoing in the old man's words.

The sun could just barely be seen above the mountains in the distance. Sunkawakan Iyopeya halted the horses near a copse. "We camp here." The woman, Julia, did not speak but slid off her pony. Shoulders hunched against the wind, she walked stiffly into the trees. Usually chattering like a magpie, she had been silent since they had left Fort Laramie. A black cloud hovered around her. He did not understand women, but he had more to worry about than one woman, no matter how important she was to him. He needed to care for their mounts and prepare the camp before darkness fell, then he would speak with her.

Later they sat in silence, the only sounds the rustle of night creatures in their hunt for food. She sat huddled in her blanket, mouth pinched, eyes shooting flames at him over the camp fire.

He was not used to explaining his actions. "Julia—"

The hairs on his neck rippled.

"Get down." He dove for his bow and arrow. A bullet stirred the air around his cheek.

She half rose, her face a twisted mask of fear and confusion.

"Get down."

The next bullet caught her in the back. She crumpled, landing inches from the flames.

He shut down the panic that threatened to seize him by the throat. Panic that he had lost his woman before he had had a chance to know her.

Bow in one hand, he crawled on his belly toward her. When he reached her still form, he covered her body with his.

The bullets had come from two different directions. He shot an arrow in the direction of the first bullet. Grabbing her by the arms, he dragged her deeper into the shelter of the trees away from the illumination of the campfire. Her breathing was rapid and shallow like the waters running over the rocks near the people's summer camp. But she was alive. She'd be safe here as he searched the area for the men who hid from him in the darkness.

He separated himself from his fear and listened. Silence, then the neigh of a horse came from the base of the outcrop to his left. Knife in one hand, he crept in the other direction.

He'd been careless, worrying about tomorrow and not alert to the dangers of today. Now the woman he'd claimed as his own might die.

The stench from the first shooter's body led Sunkawakan Iyopeya straight to him. He slit the man's throat before the shooter was aware of his presence. Warm blood still slick on his hand, he picked up the man's rifle and fired a bullet in the direction of the campfire. Hopefully, that would make the second shooter believe his partner was still alive.

Sunkawakan Iyopeya backtracked, keeping to the shadows, moving up wind of the horses. The second shooter had moved from his original position.

He'd been away from Julia too long. His heart pounded like a drum in his ears. Had the second shooter found her? Was she still alive? He took a deep breath and called on the spirits to guide him.

Hyah! Hyah!

Sunkawakan Iyopeya's head snapped around. His horses galloped off through the trees, tails high, hooves eating up the ground. Small stones clattered down the small hill as he descended the slope, heedless of the noise he made.

At the bottom of the mound just as the land met the trees, a shadow separated from the darkness. The second shooter was a Sihasapa—a Blackfoot. Probably an Indian scout. Sunkawakan Iyopeya flipped his knife so the blade faced behind him. The Blackfoot had both a pukamoggan—a club—and a knife. Arms outstretched, they circled each other. The Blackfoot bared his teeth in a grimace before he lunged. Sunkawakan Iyopeya sidestepped, spun and put a foot out to kick the Blackfoot. The Indian was quicker. Dropping his club, he grabbed Sunkawakan Iyopeya's foot, twisted it, and sent him sailing to land on his side.

Shards of pain pierced his side as if the horns of a buffalo had stabbed his body.

He sprang to his feet in time to meet the Blackfoot's oncoming rush. The Blackfoot tried to backhand Sunkawakan Iyopeya with his pukamoggan. His middle was exposed. Sunkawakan Iyopeya reared back to avoid the blow; then he moved in quickly, burying his knife in the other man's chest.

The Blackfoot sank to his knees and fell on his face, driving the knife further into his body.

Sunkawakan Iyopeya used his foot to flip the Indian over. Satisfied the Blackfoot was dead, he pulled his knife from the body, wiped the blood on the Indian's shirt and sheathed it.

The moon had started its descent in the night sky before Sunkawakan Iyopeya had finished caring for Julia's injury. He covered her with a blanket and made her as comfortable as he could and then doused the flames he had used to heat water. Julia would not survive if he could not find his horses.

The Blackfoot's mount—a fourteen hands high dark beauty—munched grass by the creek. When Sunkawakan Iyopeya approached, the roan threw back its head, eyes rolling until only the whites showed and pawed the ground.

Sunkawakan Iyopeya kept his voice low and calm. In the language of the people, he spoke to the horse of its strength, of its spirit. He approached the horse slowly, hands out by his side. The animal threw back its head and neighed. It pawed the mud at its feet, head pumping up and down as though it agreed with Sunkawakan Iyopeya's words. He whispered to the horse that his former master had selected a mighty warrior to carry him into battle and it would be an honor to be its new master. The animal pranced sideways but didn't gallop away. Sunkawakan Iyopeya laid a hand on the dappled coat, stroked the animal and then touched his forehead to the horse's and crooned softly as to a babe. "You are like moon magic, pulling the tides with your strength." The animal blew steam from its nose and bobbed its head, trying to break the spell Sunkawakan Iyopeya wound around him. Presently the roan allowed Sunkawakan Iyopeya to lead him back to where Julia lay.

Using strong tree limbs, Sunkawakan Iyopeya built a travois. Moon Magic—the name he had given the Blackfoot's mount—would pull the travois. After he had made preparations for the morning journey he stretched out next to Julia, offering her the only thing he could, his body's warmth. He didn't allow himself to drift into a deep sleep but listened to her rapid, choppy breathing and prayed to the great Wakan Tanka to keep her alive to reach his village. Once in the winter camp, the medicine man would use his magic to save her.

He jerked awake to the snap of a twig. He'd notched an arrow into his bow before his mind focused on the prairie dog sitting on its hunches, paws in the air, watching him. Though the sun was just cresting the distant peaks, the moon, pale and white, still occupied the early morning sky. Slowly he turned his attention to Julia. Her mouth was tightly drawn and a frown crinkled her forehead.

"Julia." He smoothed sweat-dampened hair from her face.

She only moaned, the sound a child made caught in an evil dream. His chest tightened. There was nothing he could do but get her to his village. But now it would take even longer, since there was only the one horse.

He rose and readied Moon Magic by tying the travois poles around the animal's neck and draped them over its back. He would walk and guide the horse. They'd been lucky. He'd found a buffalo hide, some food and extra water on the Blackfoot's horse. Sunkawakan Iyopeya filled the skins from the stream, tied them to the horse and covered Julia with the fur once he'd secured her to the travois. As the sun crested the mountains, they set off for the Lakota winter camp.

CHAPTER EIGHT

Sunkawakan Iyopeya could smell snow in the air. There had been frost the last two mornings. Now dark clouds gathered in the west.

Putting a hand on the horse's backside, he stopped Moon Magic as he'd done so many times that morning to check on Julia. He adjusted her coverings. Racked with fever, she tossed and sometimes cried out, making the horse skittish.

Sunkawakan Iyopeya studied the clouds again, and this time felt moisture on his face. They had to turn back. She would never make it if the snows and high winds came. They had passed a trapper's lodging early this morning. Maybe they could make it back to the hut before the snow.

They did not.

By the time they'd reached the hut, he was trudging through ankle-deep snow.

The lean-to was no more than long poles braced together and tied with vines. Old animal skins had been tossed over the frame, giving the interior a musty, gamey smell. There was barely enough room for him to turn around, but it was dry. He made a bed of fresh pine needles, settled Julia on them and covered her with the Blackfoot's buffalo fur. She lay limp in his arms, eyes closed and breath hot.

He hobbled Moon Magic and went in search of dry wood to make a fire. After building the blaze, he extracted his medicine pouch from his bedroll. His people used a root to cool the body and keep away the bad spirits. He ground that root with a stone and then mixed it with water until he had a thick paste. After cleaning Julia's shoulder he applied the paste and bound the area. He sat back on his heels.

Even burning with fever she was a beautiful woman. He touched her soft hair, pulling a curl and watched it spring back to her head. Reluctantly he moved from her side. She needed food and the horse needed shelter.

After snaring two rabbits, he dug a pit in the snow, built a fire and roasted some of the meat. With the remaining portion and the marrow from the bones, he made a broth in a leather pot. He dropped heated rocks into the water with the bones and marrow.

As the food cooked, he built a crude lean-to for Moon Magic. Without the horse they would die.

Later he gathered Julia into his arms and tried to get her to drink the broth. Most of the liquid dribbled from her mouth into the pine straw. He hoped some of it had reached her stomach.

The snow by this time was knee deep and falling fast. As Julia slept, he had nothing to do but think. Who had sent the two killers? His guess was the Indian agent. Fitzpatrick had not been at the fort, but word of Sunkawakan Iyopeya's visit would have reached him. Fitzpatrick probably believed, rightfully so, that Sunkawakan Iyopeya's dissatisfaction about the fate of the provisions would be spread to the tribes that signed the treaty. Enraged tribes would take out their anger on the settlers as they passed through Indian Territory. How do you head that kind of trouble off at the pass? Kill the messenger.

"Vincent?"

Julia's distressed cry drew him to her. What man's name did she call? Her mate? Did this male search for her? He drew the fur further up her body to ward off the chill. If this mate searched, he would never find her. She belonged to him now. He forgot his worries about the Indian agent and lay down next to Julia, drawing her body into the safety of his arms.

Outside the snow continued to fall.

Sunkawakan Iyopeya barely slept. Julia's thrashings woke him as soon as he drifted off. He touched her cheek. "Shhh..." Her face felt as though it had been scorched by the sun. He covered her with the fur before stepping outside.

The night was clear. The stars shone in relief against the black sky, even as the wind moaned and shook the small lean-to. He trudged through the snow to the makeshift corral. The horse had worn the ground down to mud. "You have a brave heart," he whispered to the animal. "You will be rewarded for your strength." Moon Magic neighed, tossing his head. Sunkawakan Iyopeya's prayed the Spirits would bless this journey, and he and Julia would return safely to his camp.

Her fever broke the next morning. Even though she was weak, Sunkawakan Iyopeya knew they could stay only one more day. This had been a mild storm. As the season progressed, it would get much worst.

Julia sat stiffly in the circle of Trades with Horses' arms. Each jarring step of the horse's hooves threw her against his chest, and as quickly, she moved away. At least she rode before him instead of behind him with her arms tied at the wrist like she had with Greasy Hair and Hook Nose. She glanced back at him through the curtain of her lashes. His face was expressionless, as always. There was no warmth in his eyes and his lips were tight with what? Anger? She should be grateful. He treated her with respect, even if he was cold and distant. At least he wasn't savage. Distant and cold, but not savage.

"How far to your village?" She didn't know how much longer she could stand the rattle of her bones or the nearness to his body.

"Many days ride."

This was the first time he'd spoken to her. *Ever*. She tried but failed to bring back the anger she'd felt when she learned he could speak English—and better than her. She had little memory of what happened after a bullet tore through her body. He'd nursed her that much she knew. Blushing, she glanced up at him. How much of her body had he seen? Had he seen the scars on her back? What had he thought? No matter. What mattered was she'd survived.

"Where are the horses?"

"Gone."

She waited for more of an explanation, but none came. They traveled for quite a while in silence. Lulled by the steady pace of the horse through the snow, she gave in as her lids grew heavy.

"Who is Vincent?"

Her eyes flew open, and she struggled to draw a breath. *How did he know about Vincent?* "Vincent?" Her voice croaked like a frog.

Silence greeted her question. What could she say? He was someone who'd used my body but hadn't loved me.

"Ah... Vincent be my owner." Which was true. Partially. "I be—I was a slave 'til I ran away. I ran because I wanted to be free. Free like you...like your people."

She glanced back to see his expression. His features were as smooth as stone. If not for the muscle hopping in his jaw, she would have believed he hadn't heard her—or didn't care.

They stopped frequently during the day to rest the horse. Carrying two people through heavy snow tired even a young horse like Magic Moon.

Sunkawakan Iyopeya watched for other tracks in the snow. He hoped to recapture his lost horses. He also did not want to be caught unaware by someone who wanted him dead.

His thoughts went to Julia and what she'd told him. She longed for freedom—had risked her life for it. He could understand that need. Already there was talk among the white men to corral Indians like horses on small pieces of land. They were not horses. They were the First People. They were free to live where they wanted, to hunt where they wanted. Yes, he could understand Julia's desire to be free.

She was still weak, so they camped early. He made her as comfortable as he could by a stream where a thick growth of pine trees had shed its needles. After he made a fire, he turned his attention to her wound.

She grabbed his hand when he tried to lower her dress from her shoulder. "I—I can take care of it." He looked from their clasped hands to her face. Her honey-colored eyes dropped, and she pulled her hand from beneath his.

He removed his hand from her shoulder. "I will go in search of food."

Did she not know she was his woman? His life mate? He had paid many horses for her. And because she was his, he had certain rights. No. She was too ill for him to claim *those* rights, but as soon as she was better, he would.

He dug a pit for the fire and found enough pine needles to make a comfortable bed for the two of them.

By the time the sun set he had snared rabbits, skinned and roasted them over the flames and set water to boil to cook two eggs he had found in a nest. The eggs he gave to Julia.

Later as he devoured the hot juicy rabbit, Julia eyed his meal hungrily. He did not offer her any of the meat. It was too soon. Her stomach would rebel.

After he finished eating, he scooped up a handful of snow and rubbed the grease off his fingers. Julia stared at the remaining meat as she nibbled an egg.

"Why did you escape by yourself?"

She stopped eating but did not look at him. "Because I was stupid."

He waited.

The wind moaned through the pines and snow drifted out of the trees to land at Moon Magic's feet. The horse threw back its head and whinnied.

"Bo—" Jumping up, she tossed the egg into the flames before and stalking off toward the trees. She swiped at her face, stared at the woods for several moments and then came back to her position by the fire. "He wanted to come..." She shook her head. "But they'd have cut off his foot this time." She rubbed again at her face with the palms of her hands. "I couldn't let that happen."

Sunkawakan Iyopeya shifted uneasily. Women of his tribe did not show this emotion, at least not outside their teepee.

"I snuck away." She did not say more, and he did not ask.

The horse whinnied, drawing her attention. She pointed at Moon Magic. "Whose horse is that?"

Before he could answer, she asked another question. "Who shot me?" Her voice quivered.

He poked a stick into the fire. Sparks shot into the air before disappearing back into the pit. He looked at her then back at the flames. "We should not have gone to the fort."

"Why?"

"I angered the Indian agent." He rose and threw more branches on the fire. Embers shot up into the night sky. "He probably thought I would stir up trouble."

"Would you?"

"Yes."

If he had known someone would come after him, he would have taken Julia to his camp and then gone to the fort. His decision filled him with remorse. If he had lost her...

He glanced over to where she sat. Her chin rested on her chest. He went to her and lifted her into his arms. "It is time for you to rest."

She stared up at him with sleepy brown eyes. "Where will you bed down?"

He hesitated, staring at the pine needles he had fashioned into a bed, envisioning how soft they would be. How warm her body would be next to his. "Over there." He indicated a place near Moon Magic. A place heavy with snow and surrounded by pines whose branches were laden with more snow. "I will bed down there."

He placed her gently on the blanket that covered the needles and stalked across the camp to his bed. It was as cold and wet as he had envisioned.

The hoot of an owl brought Julia out of a cold, restless sleep. The campfire's embers still glowed in the pit, and the sky was as dark as when she'd lain down. She clamped her teeth together to still their chattering. The pine needles had been flattened by her shifting in her sleep. It felt as though every stone in the woods had come to rest under her back.

She sat up and tucked her frozen feet under her body. Horseman was a lump against the darkness—a warm lump. She remembered his body heat as they'd ridden on Moon Magic the last two days. The man could set wood on fire without rubbing two sticks together.

What would he think if she came willing to his sleeping spot? She'd been aware he slept by her side when they were at the cabin, but she'd been so lost in her pain, she hadn't cared.

No. She couldn't do it. She wrapped the buffalo skin around her body and curled up tighter on the ground. A rock the size of a boulder dug into her right side. She flipped over. The snow around the fire had melted and the water had run downhill straight into her bed.

She glared at Horseman sleeping so peacefully on his side of the fire. Why would she want to sleep beside him? He'd never told her what happened the night she was attacked. She remembered her time with Greasy Hair and the Indians who'd first captured her. They were a bloodthirsty bunch. Horseman had probably killed the men who'd shot her. She tried to close her mind to how he killed them, but she couldn't. Imagines of the farmer and his family being scalped flashed behind her closed lids. Her gut twisted.

No, it was best she stay on her side of the fire. To take her mind off the cold, she thought about being in the cane fields with the sun beating on her back—her back cut to shreds by the overseer's whip.

Horseman wasn't like Greasy Hair. Silent and hard, he'd probably killed, but he'd paid many horses for her and rescued her from that slavery. He hadn't tied her up in the many days they'd been together and never tried to force himself on her. She could trust him. What choice did she have? She was probably many miles from the North and between here and there were many white men.

Rising, she limped on cold feet across the space of the camp to Horseman's sleeping pallet. Without uttering a word, she stretched out beside him and spread the buffalo fur across them both.

She closed her eyes and thought about warm summer nights and imagined the sounds of the bullfrogs coming from the bayou. Little by little the coldness seeped from her bones until she was limp and her eyelids heavy. In her dreams, he gathered her close to his body.

Several days later Julia stomped up and down the banks of a large river. Every time she glanced at the angry waves her heart would bang against her chest. The water was dark like the sky before a storm. There was no way she was gonna cross that river. Even the crazy animal Horseman called Moon Magic agreed with her. Its eyes rolled until only the whites showed. Horseman would have to cross without her.

"The river is full from the melting of the snows," he said.

"I cross when it dries up."

The tightness of his lips told Julia he'd heard her. "My village lies on the other side of this river. We have to cross."

Her gut twisted and churned like the dark water raging in front of her. "You can't make me cross that river."

His gaze was rock hard, eyes narrowed. "We *will* cross."

"Can't swim," she said under her breath. Her heart beat faster just thinking about moving out into the water.

"You will be on Moon Magic."

"What?" Her mouth was as dry as the cane field after harvest. "That animal is as scared as me." As though it understood her words, the crazy horse pawed the mud, repeatedly with his right leg. "What if I fall off?"

"Hold on to the reins, and you will be fine." He pointed to the two horses he'd recaptured that were hobbled nearby. "I'll take one over and come back for the second horse. When you ride Moon Magic across, I'll be close behind."

Julia snorted. She closed her eyes and did something she hadn't done since her mother was alive. She prayed.

When Horseman tried to lead the second horse toward the water's edge, the animal sidestepped then backed up. Horseman stroked its head and whispered something only the two of them could hear. Julia shook her head in wonder. The Indian talked more to the horses than he'd spoken to her during the whole trip.

He beckoned. Her heart pounded in time to the water battering over the rocks. He held the horse steady. It took two tries, but she mounted, straightened her back and tightened the reins with a sweaty grip. Their gazes locked.

His black eyes surrounded by water-clumped lashes were steady on hers. He nodded once, a nod that said you-can-do-it. She took a deep breath and nudged the horse toward the water.

The water flowed fast, but it only came up to the horse's knees. She relaxed. Horseman would be close behind her, everything would be fine. She loosened her death grip on the reins.

As the horse moved toward the middle of the river, the water started to creep up. The icy fingers of the river rushed over her leg and kept rising. "Yea, though I walk through the valley of the shadow of death, I will fear no evil," she mumbled the prayer as she kept her eyes on the opposite shore. Moon Magic's head bobbed as he made his way across the river.

The water rose over her knees. Her breath came in ragged pants.

Moon Magic let out an ear-piercing whinny.

Julia forgot to breathe. Charging toward them, as wild as the horse's eyes, was a wave of high water.

"Oh, Lord, be with me in this hour of—"

The wall of water hit, tossing Julia off the horse into the river. The icy river closed over her head, gushing through her nose and ears. Her heart and breathing stopped as she sank through the murky depths. She didn't want to die. She had too much to live for. Teaching in the North. Freedom.

She flailed her arms and kicked her feet, but her body dropped like a stone. She struggled to hold her breath as fish and tree limbs flew past. Her lungs ached with the need to expand and take in air. Black dots appeared in her vision. She hit bottom so hard, she felt she'd broken something. But the thud shot her back toward the surface. Her body wanted to breathe. The need to take in air was great. She frantically kicked toward the top.

Hurry. Hurry. The surface was just ahead. Light. Salvation. But she was going blind. Blackness took over her sight until all she saw was a little tiny whole of light. Her body screamed for air. *Hurry.*

Just when she thought she couldn't hold her breath a moment longer, she broke the surface of the water. She dragged air into her tortured lungs. Flailing wildly to keep herself afloat, she took in more water than air. The force of the current spun and beat at her body harder than any whip. She didn't have time to take in her surroundings before the river claimed her again, pulling her down into its depths. This time she kicked and pushed her body upward and broke the surface again. Something flashed in the corner of her eye. Pain, hot and black as death, exploded in her head.

Sunkawakan Iyopeya dove into the icy river. One moment Julia had been in front of him on the back of Moon Magic and the next she was gone. Beneath the raging surface all he could see was dead fish and tree limbs.

He turned in circles, kicking his feet as his eyes strained against the watery dimness. No Julia.

He broke the surface and swam with the current instead of against it as he surveyed the banks. Moon Magic peacefully grazed on the opposite side.

Swimming to the bank, he crawled out of the water. He gathered Moon Magic's reins and galloped down the river in the direction of the current. He abandoned the horse and dove into the river again and again.

When he was too tired to swim, he floated on the current until it deposited him on the shore.

CHAPTER NINE

"Well, lookee here. She's back from the dead."

Julia had been attempting to open her eyes, but at the sound of that voice, she stopped. Frozen in fear, she lay on cold, wet ground and held her breath. *Lord, no. It can't be.*

"Don't play like you don't hear me, girly." Jack Murphy's voice was close to her face, breath smelling like something had curled up and died in his mouth. "I've been chasing your black ass all over this country for the last four months. 'Magine my surprise when you came floating down that river. Right into my arms." His laughter sounded like the bray of a jackass.

How had he found her? And where was Horseman? He was supposed to be behind her. She remembered gasping for air after struggling up from the bottom of the river and then nothing.

"Wake up, bitch." The overseer kicked her in the gut.

Fire lashed through her body, scorching everywhere it touched. She wretched, bringing up river water.

Through a haze of white-hot pain, she heard another voice, one she didn't recognize.

"Need to get going. That red savage has to be around somewhere."

Horseman. They knew about Horseman. Had they been following her? For how long?

She pushed through the pain, forcing her eyes open. She couldn't wait on Horseman to save her. What if he didn't come?

They were not far from the river. She could hear its roar, and the wind brought the smell of wet earth and dead fish. They were in a clearing but surrounded by woods. The ash from a fire twirled in the wind. Movement sounded behind her but she was too tired and in too much pain to turn around.

The overseer mounted his horse, a reddish brown animal. "Hand her up."

Hands locked around her body and lifted her into Jack Murphy's waiting arms. The overseer flashed a tobacco-stained smile as he tied her wrists together. "Thought you could run from me, huh?" He tightened the rope until it bite into her flesh. "Well, ain't no way I coulda gone back to the plantation without you—and not with high and mighty Vincent dead."

Visions of Vincent's bloody scalp flashed behind her closed lids. She shuddered.

"Yes, siree. Mistress Donnelly is gonna love me now. I done brought back her prize gal." He said the words like he could easily have switched mule for gal.

He pushed her face down so she hung hogtied, her nose mashed into the horse's side. She turned her head so she could breathe more than the hay smell coming off the animal.

Murphy's meaty fingers stroked her backside. "Always thought you were a fine piece."

Blackness filled Julia's mind. He was taking her back to the plantation. No freedom for her. After they beat her, Mistress Donnelly would bury her so far in the cane field she'd never see daylight again. If she didn't sell her. Tears leaked from Julia's eyes. She'd come so far.

The slow steady sway and clop of the horse hooves made her head throb. Closing her eyes made the dizziness worse. She gritted her teeth against the pain and sickness.

She wouldn't let them take her back. She'd rather die.

They rode forever. The near drowning, the fear, the lack of hope was too much. Somehow she slept. She woke when the horse stopped moving. Dusk had fallen.

Murphy dragged her off the horse. She landed on her ass. The fall made her teeth snap together. Her shoulder had ached all day from the unnatural position across the back of the horse, and the pulling on the tender flesh around the gunshot wound. Hands still tied together, she struggled to her feet, her moccasins slippery on the damp earth.

Through the leafless trees, she could see a river rushing past. Was it the same one she almost drowned in earlier in the day?

The overseer's buddy led the horses down to the river to drink. For the first time she got a look at the man. Tall, thin with a wide brimmed hat that hid his face, he walked with his shoulders hunched against the cold.

The ground was still wet in spots from the heavy snows, which explained why Murphy cursed a blue streak as he gathered firewood. Everything on the ground was probably wet. She smiled to herself. At least she wasn't being worked like a slave. He probably thought she'd run if he'd given her that task. And she would have.

Later, he untied her hands to eat the burnt beans and salt pork. The food sat on her stomach like a river rock, but she had to have strength to escape, so she ate.

Murphy's partner glanced at her as he shoveled food into his mouth. "Long way from Nebraskee to Louisiana. How we gonna get her back?" He sopped up the remaining food on his tin plate with grimy fingers. "Injuns everywhere and plenty of men who'd gladly take her off our hands for the money."

Murphy belched. "We travel by the river. One of us will sleep and the other guard. That's the best way."

Putting down his tin plate, he stretched out his legs as he settled back on his bedroll. Closing his eyes, he said, "You take the first watch."

"What about her?"

"Tie her up. She ain't going nowhere."

The Scarecrow, as she called him, tied her wrist together behind a tree. She gritted her teeth against the pain in her shoulder.

As he walked away, she shouted after him, "I need a blanket." Still wet from her near drowning in the river and too far from the campfire to feel any heat, she'd freeze without covering.

When neither man spoke, she said, "Mistress Donnelly ain't gonna pay you if I'm dead from the ague."

The overseer lifted his hat from his face, squinted at her and turned over so his beefy back was warmed by the fire. The Scarecrow walked off into the trees.

Tucking her legs as close to her body as she could, Julia leaned back against the tree. She must have slept, because she woke to a hand twisting her breast.

"Well now, girly, I think you owe me something." He straightened her legs before running a beefy hand from her knee to the junction of her thighs. "You give that Injun some of this?" He palmed her private parts, smiling a smile that was slimier than a pig's innards.

She'd been cold earlier, but now her skin felt hot and her mouth dry—not from fear but fury. "Maybe."

She got a spark of pleasure at seeing his blue eyes darken with anger. His face, always red, now turned almost purple.

He backhanded her.

Black spots danced before her eyes and her ears rang like the call to service on Sunday morning. Her hair caught in the rough bark of the pine tree, making her eyes tear.

"Crawford," Murphy called, never taking his gaze off Julia.

So that was Scarecrow's name.

"Yeah," Crawford answered back.

"Keep your eyes open, man." The overseer turned his attention back to Julia, spreading her thighs.

She bucked and tried kicking him. "Get your filthy—"

He grasped her chin in his meaty paw and licked her face with a thick warm tongue. Her skin prickled.

Laughing, he set back on his heels. "I ain't gonna stick nothin' in your mouth to get it bit off."

Still smiling, he unbuttoned his pants—pants stiff with mud and day's old grime. He reached inside and stroked his manhood. "I'm gonna give—"

Murphy jerked. He stared at her for a long second and then dropped on her like a boulder.

An arrow, still quivering, stuck out of his back. He took one long shuddering breath and went still.

Heart stuttering in her chest, Julia bit back a scream. Her gaze flew from one tree to another. Were they being attacked by Indians? Nothing moved.

Squirming, she tried to twist from beneath the dead man. He seemed heavier in death. She dug in her heels, pushing and straining and fighting down the terror that climbed up her throat. Where was Crawford? Did she dare scream?

Her vision was suddenly blocked by a shadow that came between her and the fire. She couldn't see the face. A bow and arrow hung down by the man's side. His shoulders were broader. His scent was familiar. Mouth dry, she couldn't form words. Didn't dare hope.

"Horseman?" Her voice seemed to be carried away with the wind.

"Vermin," he said as he pulled the overseer's body off her.

She started to cry. She never cried. But she couldn't help herself. He was such a welcome sight. He pulled his knife from its sheath and cut the rope that bound her to the tree. She'd been in the position so long she couldn't move her arms. He massaged her hands and arms and then placed them at her side. Tiny pricks like ant bites nibbled at her skin.

He sat on his haunches and studied her. She stopped rubbing her arms and glanced wildly around. Where was the other one?

"Dead."

Face expressionless, Horseman stared at her until she understood. "Oh." The overseer had been so blinded by his lust he hadn't realized it wasn't Scarecrow who answered him.

Horseman lifted her to her feet. "Come, let us leave this place."

Moon Magic neighed at the scent and sight of her. Grateful to not be heading back to the Louisiana plantation, she forgave the horse for dumping her into the river and almost causing her death.

Julia looked around. "Where are the other horses?"

"Gone."

He didn't go into more detail, but mounted Moon Magic, and pulled her up to ride behind him. As they rode away, she leaned back into his warmth, not ashamed of her need for his comfort. For the first time since her mother had died, she felt at peace.

They rode for the rest of the night only stopping once to allow Moon Magic to eat and drink. Julia didn't want food or sleep. She only wanted to put as much distance as possible between her and the scene of death back at the campsite.

While Moon Magic drank from a stream, Julia studied the moon as it started its descent. She could feel Horseman's gaze on her. Turning, she faced him boldly. She owed him the courtesy of looking him in the eye. "Thank you," she said quietly.

He only nodded, before turning his attention back to the horse.

"You didn't have to come after me. I know I've been trouble."

He squatted and ran a hand over the horse's forelegs. She could sense the awareness in his body and knew she had his full attention. It was his way to not say much and she could appreciate that about him.

"I thought my life was over back there." She pointed in the direction they'd come, even though he wasn't looking at her. "Funny, I was at peace when I thought I'd die in that river, but being rutted on by that—" she spat the bad taste out of her mouth "—that pig was worse than death."

Horseman stared out over the dark river. Flowing softly over the rocks in its bed, the water was calm now, gurgling as it flowed along its course.

"That man you shot with the arrow, he was the boss man back on—back where I came from." She too stroked Moon Magic. It was as though the horse provided comfort for both of them. His strong muscles quivered under her touch.

"You have so much freedom here." She pointed to the land that surrounded them. "You come and go when you want. No one tells you do this or do that. No one—" she'd almost said, "no one uses your body for their pleasure without asking." But she wasn't ready to say those things to him. He was a strong man. A proud man. The women in his tribe were probably as strong. She remembered the Indian women in the two camps where she'd been held. Those woman spoke their minds. They wouldn't let a man use them and then throw them away when someone better and more acceptable came along.

"I was Mistress' property—like a mule, a horse." Tears pricked her eyes. She took a deep breath. *Be strong, girl.* "Don't want to be somebody's property. Wanna be my own woman."

Still squatting, Horseman stared up at her. "You are my woman."

Fear clutched at Julia throat. Here it was, what she'd been afraid of—him wanting to own her. "About that..." How could she tell him she couldn't be a bedmate to him? He was a fine specimen of a man. He had courage, strength, and there was a gentleness to his spirit. But if she lay with him, he would want her to stay. And she couldn't stay.

As though sensing her fears, he stood up abruptly. "Time to go. The sun will be up soon."

She caught him by the arm as he moved past her. "Horseman—"

"Sunkawakan Iyopeya," he stated.

She stumbled over his name. "Sun..." She flushed, glad that in the dark he couldn't see her face. "What does all that mean?"

"He who trades with horses."

"Trades with Horses," she muttered. "That fits. I'll call you that, 'til I can say your name."

He gathered Moon Magic's reins. "We must go."

They rode all that day and well into the evening. When they finally stopped to make camp, Julia almost fell off the horse's back. Her legs felt as bowed as Horseman—Trades with Horses'—weapon as she stumbled into the woods to do her business. When she returned, Trades with Horses had disappeared. Moon Magic feasted on something green that had escaped the snows. Figuring Trades with Horses had gone hunting, Julia sank to the forest floor, propped her back against a pine tree and closed her eyes. The horse would let her know if someone approached their little camp.

The smell of roasting meat woke her. She settled on a log and took the meat Trades with Horses offered her. The flavor was so good she smacked her lips in pleasure. "What we eating? You find a chicken somewhere?"

"Snake."

Her stomach heaved, trying to bring up the food she'd already swallowed. She spit out what was in her mouth.

Trades with Horses passed her the pouch. She snatched it and guzzled down the water.

Turning an evil eye on him, she said, "Snake? We eating snake?"

His strong teeth bit with enjoyment into the flesh. He didn't answer just licked the juices off his lips. She turned away. Didn't Indians have no sense? Didn't they know snakes were poison? She'd barely survived the snakebite she gotten in the bayou.

She took a slow, deep breath, afraid to give her stomach any reason to send the offending meal back up. What she wouldn't give for some sassafras tea.

The thought of the hot brew made her think of her family—Bo, old Bessie and Cook. Julia could be eating the leftovers from Mistress Donnelly's dinner table: crawfish stew or chicken and greens. How she loved herself some greens and skillet bread. She could almost taste the pot liquor from the greens. Okay maybe that wasn't a good idea. Her gut still hadn't settled. She took another swig from the water skin.

Finished with his meal, Trades with Horses rose and went to check on Moon Magic. Julia immediately forgot about the snake. It would be time to rest for the night. Where would he sleep?

Trades with Horses settled down in a spot not far from the fire. She sat on the opposite side of the flames and thought about her situation. If she ran, she'd never make it off the Plains without him. Probably freeze to death. She clinched her fists. Who was she fooling? She might not want to be his woman, but she enjoyed the warmth of his body. Being close to him at night kept her from thinking about all the animals out there.

Sighing, she picked up her fur and settled down beside him. She gave him her back rather than spooning with him as they'd done on the nights she healed. Back to back meant they shared body heat and nothing more.

The woman Julia tossed and turned until the moon rose high in the sky. Women's minds were always a mystery to him, but it didn't take a medicine man to know something kept her from rest. Turning, Sunkawakan Iyopeya laid a hand on her shoulder. "We have a long ride tomorrow."

She tensed like an animal catching the scent of a hunter.

He removed his hand and rolled onto his back. Stars blazed in the clear night sky.

"When I was a boy, I'd take my bow and travel to the top of the tallest mountain. I'd watch the stars make their journey across the sky. Before they'd completed their voyage, I'd drift off to sleep."

She turned onto her back, and he felt the tension ease out of her body.

"Didn't pay much attention to the stars. Not much time for star-watching when you're bone-weary," she said.

They lay in silence, shoulders barely touching.

"You know much about them stars?"

"Some." Memories of his youth and innocence flashed in his mind, the days when he and his friends would sleep in the mountains secure in the knowledge they belonged to the land and it would always be their home. All his innocence ended when his older brother was killed by the white soldiers.

"The Creator, Wakan Tanka, made the universe, including the stars. We learned as boys to navigate using those stars. With the Great Spirit surrounding us, we thought we could conquer the world."

She sighed. In that release of breath, he heard a lifetime of longing.

"I wish my family could see all this."

They lay side by side while the moon inched across the sky. Her warmth and the fur made him drowsy.

"Mama, Bessie, Bo, and Cook—they'd love being here—here in this wide-open place. They'd love to sleep under the stars." She pulled the fur to her chin.

He wanted to gather her against him. His fingers twitched to pull at the curls that framed her face, but he didn't move. She was like a fawn. One sudden move and she'd flee, hidden from him by the foliage of her fears.

"Do you have family?" Her voice was a whisper in his ear.

The heat of their combined warmth made his limbs loose and his mind slow and slumberous. Not an unpleasant feeling. "I have a mother, father and one sister."

She sighed. "Wish I had a sister."

Laughter erupted from his belly. "You can have mine."

She rose up on one elbow, and frowning, stared into his face. "I can't—" Her face broke into a half smile. "You funnin' with me?"

A fur trapper had married one of the women of their tribe and taught Sunkawakan Iyopeya many words, so he had a good understanding of the white man's language. But this word...

"Funnin?" he repeated.

"You really wanna give her away?"

He paused as he thought about his sister. "She is like the prairie dog who has no hunger but digs up nuts you have planted for safekeeping. So, yes, sometimes I want to give her away."

He could barely see her face in the darkness, but he sensed the stillness of her body. "Do you love her?"

"Love?"

She cocked her head and her gaze worried his face. "Do you know the meaning of that word?"

"I've heard it. It is a white man's word. But do I understand it...?" He studied the stars for a long moment. "No, I do not."

She reached out a hand to touch his chest but hastily drew it back. He wanted to grab it and place it on his body. Lust he understood.

"Do you love someone?" *Did she love this Vincent?*

She was silent so long he thought she'd fallen asleep.

"No. I only loved my mama." Julia sighed. "Gone last winter."

He thought of his own mother—that woman who was always after him to choose a mate. The woman who

brought every unmated female in their village to his tent—
and some from outside their village. She didn't want to
understand he would pick a mate when the time was right
and when the right female spoke to him.

Now, listening to the deep breathing of the woman who
lay next to him, he knew as he had back in To'too' he's
camp, he'd found that woman.

CHAPTER TEN

"We'll camp here for the night," Trades with Horses said.

Here was a rocky outcrop of reddish clay. There were no streams and no trees. Brown grasses dead from the winter snows sprouted between the rocks. The wind howled, whipping the grass to and fro.

Julia removed the bedrolls from their mounts before Trades with Horses led them off to feed. While he hobbled the horses, she gathered bits of buffalo dung to build a fire. As they ate the last of the deer meat and drank water that tasted like the skin it had been stored in, the sun's rays disappeared behind the Black Hills or Paha Sapa, as Trades with Horses called them. One minute the sun's rays cast long shadows across the land and the next, she couldn't see beyond the glow of the campfire.

"Tell me about your village."

He poked the dying embers of the fire. "During the winter, the tribe divides into small groups and follows the buffalo. When we join my father's camp, there will be about twenty or thirty men, women and children."

"Your father's camp?"

"My father is the tribal chief."

She thought of Vincent and Mistress Donnelly who were chiefs of their land. Would his father look down on her with displeasure because she'd been a slave?

"Will you be the next chief?" She watched his face closely.

He shrugged, staring into the fire as though it could foretell the future. "Each chief is elected. It is an honor that is earned."

She'd seen his concern about the provisions promised to the other tribes, his worry that there won't be enough food. He would make a good chief.

"But you want to be the next chief?"

He hesitated. "I'm not sure."

She had another question to ask him now that they were talking so openly to each other.

He'd called her his woman, but she'd thought she was Vincent's woman. She'd been wrong. He'd brought home a wife. Would that happen again with Trades with Horses?

She stared at the flames and couldn't meet his eyes, but she had to know now. "Do...do you have a wife?"

"Wife?" His thick brows drew together.

"A woman. Someone who shares your sleeping mat." Julia held her breath. As much as she didn't want to admit it, this was important. She would not be someone's second woman. She couldn't believe she was thinking these thoughts. Not when she had no intention of staying past spring.

"I do not have someone who shares my sleeping mat."

Julia almost sagged in relief but caught herself. She wouldn't let him know how important his answer had been.

Rising, he threw the last of the dung on the fire. Sparks and smoke shot into the air. "It is time for bed. Tomorrow we will arrive in my camp." He stalked off to a place just outside the fire light.

Julia didn't move. She should be happy the end of the journey was near, but her gut cramped like she'd eaten bad meat. She'd grown comfortable being with him, the horses and the ever-changing land. Once they reached his village, she'd have to share him with his family and the rest of the tribe. As much as she wanted to deny it, she'd come to enjoy his company, his nearness.

Fiery sparks glowed in the dark. After staring for a few more minutes into the flames, she rose and walked toward his bed. He wasn't asleep but waited for her. He opened the fur and when she'd settled down beside him, he drew her into his warmth.

Eyes closed, she enjoyed his closeness. When spring came, she'd be gone and would never know this peace again.

The sun had almost dropped behind the mountain range when they arrived in his people's camp.

Sunkawakan Iyopeya leapt off his horse, energy racing through his body. It had been a long journey—longer for Julia.

She didn't protest when he took Moon Magic's reins from her hands and guided the horse

toward his mother's teepee. The days since the shooting and crossing the Great River had been hard on her. He would let her rest while he impressed on his father the importance of calling a meeting of the elders. They needed a plan to make it through the snowy season.

The camp was usually filled with activity at this time of day, yet today it was quiet. Yes, it was cold, but that didn't mean there weren't horses to feed, hides to clean.

He whipped aside the flap to his mother's teepee and stepped into the dark interior. Words of greeting died on his lips as a low keening filled the air. A cold knot formed in his gut, sending its icy tentacles to invade the rest of his body. Two people stood over one lying on a pallet. The stench of death was like a living thing in the lodge.

He stalked over to the pallet. Words locked in his throat. His father lay still as a stone, his skin as gray as shale. His mother rocked back and forth—each motion threatening to send her face first onto his father's still form. Eyes closed, the medicine man, Matosapa, sang a song of healing under his breath. They seemed unaware of his presence.

He dropped to his knees beside the pallet and touched his father's shoulder. The old man's eyes opened slowly. For a brief moment a spark of light brightened his gaze.

"Son…" His father extended a trembling hand.

Sunkawakan Iyopeya took his father's cold, thin fingers in his. How had this happened? His father had been hearty when he had left the village at the end of summer.

"Rest." He laid a calming hand on his father's arm.

"You must be—" a cough cut off his words "—chief."

He shook his head. "No, Father. You are chief. This illness will pass." Even as he said the

words, in his heart, he knew the truth. Thin and wasted, his father would not leave his bed. The Great Spirit would take him away to ride the foothills before the new moon.

His mother sank to her knees beside the pallet. Haggard and just as thin as her husband, she rocked to and fro, silent now in her grief.

When his father's hand grew slack, Sunkawakan Iyopeya rose and signaled to the medicine man to follow him outside.

In the brief time he had been inside the teepee, he had forgotten it was winter and cold, forgotten that the air could smell crisp with snow, forgotten that life still continued with the calling of the hawks over the land.

The tribal members huddled in small groups, whispering. They grew silent as he searched their familiar faces. These were his people. People who would need guidance in the treacherous waters that lay ahead. Who among them could lead if his father died?

The sight of Julia brought him back from his dark thoughts. Holding the horses' reins, she stood perfectly composed and regal, even in her worn and stained deerskin dress. She smiled at him and for the moment his world righted, until the Shaman's solid hand landed on his shoulder, reminding him of his father's impending death.

"Sunkawakan Iyopeya." Matosapa beckoned him away from the mouth of the tent.

"Wait." He walked back to Julia's side.

Her big honey-colored eyes roamed his face. "What's wrong?"

He took the reins of the horses from her and signaled for one the young men to take the animals away.

"My father—" His lips had no feeling. If he gave birth to the words, it would be so. "My father is—ill."

She laid a hand over his and squeezed. Her eyes said how sorry she was. Even though the top of her head only reached his chin, he wanted to lean into her strength, bury his face in her neck and forget what lay ahead.

Aware the whole village watched, he took a deep breath and made his way back to Matosapa.

Frowning, the medicine man studied Julia. Without saying a word, he turned and led Sunkawakan Iyopeya toward a grove of trees. "Who is that woman?" He asked when they were a distance away from the tribal members.

"Julia."

Dark eagle eyes bore into Sunkawakan Iyopeya's. "She will be your second woman?"

It was not forbidden among his people to have more than one woman, but it complicated lives and he did not want complications. He wanted one woman—Julia.

"She is my one and only woman."

Those words brought the medicine man's piercing gaze back to his face. "What of—"

"What is wrong with my father?" Sunkawakan Iyopeya didn't have time for the niceties of words he normally would have encouraged.

"He is dying." Matosapa said.

A pain sharp as a blade dug into Sunkawakan Iyopeya's ribs and up to his heart. "There is no medicine—"

"He has been dying for many moons. He has kept his own counsel. But now there's no more time."

Sunkawakan Iyopeya turned and stared at his mother's teepee as though the strength of his connection to his father would make the old man rise strong from his pallet.

"We must choose another chief."

Sunkawakan Iyopeya opened his mouth to protest, but he had seen the condition of his father's body and spirit.

His father had been a strong leader. He alone believed the visions his son had had of their people's fate at the hands of the white man. Against the wishes of the medicine man, his father had allowed him to speak at the council of the elders. He and his father had made an enemy of Matosapa, but Sunkawakan Iyopeya never doubted the medicine man's ability. His predictions in the past had been true. But in this one prediction Matosapa's vision had been clouded by the belief the Indian peoples were invincible. They weren't.

Sunkawakan Iyopeya had hoped with time, and his father's support, he could make the council believe. But time had run out.

He nodded. "Yes, there must be a calling of the elders of the tribe." He couldn't call a meeting, but the medicine man could.

"You could be chief," Matosapa said.

Although he respected the medicine man, he did not believe Matosapa always had the ear of the Great Spirit. "It would take an agreement of tribal members for one man to be elected."

The medicine man looked back toward the circle of teepees. Sunkawakan Iyopeya followed the direction of his gaze. Julia stood as he'd left her, hands folded, serene and beautiful.

"I could speak on your behalf."

For one moment, the band around Sunkawakan Iyopeya's chest eased. For one moment, he forgot that Matosapa was his enemy. He might be able prevent the bloodshed of so many of his people. But he detected the gleam of cold calculation in the old man's eyes.

"Why would you do this?"

Matosapa's smile was cold. "Because I have the interest of the tribe at heart. I know you would make the best chief." He paused, his eyes boring into Sunkawakan Iyopeya. "With my daughter at your side as your *only* wife."

Julia woke to the crackle of a small fire burning in a pit in the middle of the hut. The teepee was empty. She thought back to the previous evening. She'd met so many people and heard so many names—none of which she could say. Some had been friendly, but some had watched her with cold stares. One of those unwelcoming people had been Trades with Horses' sister, whose teepee Julia now slept in.

She stood, straightened her pallet before stepping outside. The weak sun had barely crested the mountains, leaving frost on the hard packed ground. She wrapped a blanket around her shoulders against the wild wind that still blew from the west.

The camp was eerily quiet, causing a chill to run up her back that had nothing to do with the wind.

A long shrill wail pierced the air.

A mutt who'd had his nose to the ground in search of food a moment ago, let loose a howl that hurt her ears.

People rushed from their lodgings and stood in huddled silence staring at Trades with Horses' teepee. After a long moment, he stepped out. He spoke to the people. Before he'd stopped speaking more wails filled the air. Some of the women began to tear at their hair and clothing. Julia knew this grief. She could feel it in her bones. Her people expressed their loss in this way and she felt at home with this outpouring of sorrow.

How did she comfort Trades with Horses? Would he welcome her words, her touch? Watching his face for some

sign of displeasure, she walked to his side and placed a
hand on his arm. "Your father...?"

"Is dead." His eyes were cold and distant.

She wanted to wrap her arms around him, but the men
she knew—the ones on the plantation—didn't welcome
that kind of comfort. They were quick to take some woman
to their pallets, but they didn't want to be soothed when
their pain was unbearable.

She and Trades with Horses were still strangers. She'd
shared his blanket, their bodies touching in sleep, but
they'd never shared their hearts.

Arms wrapped tightly around her body instead of his,
Julia whispered, "I'm sorry." He nodded, his face as
smooth as the surface of a calm lake, his eyes dark and
troubled as a gathering storm. He turned and stepped back
into his family's teepee. Not knowing what to do and
feeling as useless as a broken wagon wheel, she found her
way down to the creek. There she sat on a rock and lilted
her face to the sun and allowed it to warm her cold body.

Her journey was far different from what she'd pictured
when she'd run from the plantation last summer. She was
as far from her destination as when she'd sat on the stoop
of her mother's little shack. It would be easy for her to take
one of the horses and leave this camp. No one would know
or even care. So wrapped up in his grief, Trades with
Horses wouldn't realize she'd left for several days. For
some reason that made her sad. Sad her presence meant so
little. She blinked against the tears. *Can't have it both
ways, gal.*

Should she go or should she stay?

Pebbles trickled down the path as a young Indian
woman made her way to the creek.

Slender with a single black braid that hung down her
back, the woman seemed lost in her own thoughts as she
walked to the water's edge. She didn't speak to Julia just
stared out over the creek. The sun now higher sent beams
dancing across the grey-blue surface. This would be a

beautiful and peaceful spot during the warm months, and Julia could understand the woman's need to seek comfort here.

Not wanting to disturb her, Julia rose to go back to camp. If their gazes met, she was prepared to offer a warm smile and greeting. Trades with Horses had taught her a few words in his language. That smile was already forming on her lips, when the Indian woman stepped into her path. Their gazes locked and the smile died on Julia's lips. The expression that blazed from the woman's eyes made her stumble backwards. Anger? Hatred?

The woman reached out and stopped Julia's backward slide. Her fingers dug into Julia's arm like eagle talons.

"Sunkawakan Iyopeya mithawa" The woman beat on her chest. Julia understood the gesture even if she hadn't understood the word. This woman had told her that Trades with Horses belonged to her.

The woman forcibly released Julia's arm, causing her to stumbled, slide and fall to her knees.

Breathless with her heart thudding in her ears, Julia stood. She ignored the pain in her hands and knees as she watched the young woman disappear into the trees at the top of the rise. Anger caught her by the throat. While Trades with Horses was proclaiming his desire for her, he'd failed to tell her another woman had rights to his heart. Were all men alike? Gatherin' women like berries from a bush. The woman could have Trades with Horses. As soon the snows cleared Julia would leave. Gathering her dignity around her, she slowly climbed the path back to the village.

Julia had a chance to look upon the chief's face for the first and only time just before they raised him to a platform built high off the ground. Even in death, the father looked very much like the son. She gazed at the old man's features and branded them to memory so she'd know what Trades with Horses would look like when he was older—when she'd no longer be with him.

Trades with Horses stood apart from the other mourners. Like the eye of a storm, he was the calm center to the whirling madness of the other tribal members. They'd cut their hair, torn their clothes, and to Julia's horror, some were hacking off their fingertips. Only the black stripes of paint on Trades with Horses' face showed his sorrow.

She knew his pain. Losing her mama had been the hardest thing that had happened in her life. She thought of her mama's grave with her name—Mae—scratched on a small stone marker. As long as Bo was alive or not sold off, Julia knew he would take care of her mama's grave and put flowers on the ground for her birthday.

At least Trades with Horses still had his mother, even if, she was like a leech, sucking and pulling all his strength from him. Maybe Julia was being unfair. Maybe his mother was just broken down in her grief. But who was holding Trades with Horses up in his time of sorrow? Where was this young woman who said she loved him? Julia didn't see her in the sea of faces. As angry as she was with him for not telling her about this woman, she felt his sorrow for the loss of his father.

As though her feet had a mind of their own, she walked to his side. She didn't touch or speak to him but stood silently beside him, lending him her strength.

The ceremony lasted long into the night. Fires had been built around the platform that held the chief. Trades with Horses didn't moved, just watched the mourners dance and wail. Tired and cold, Julia shifted her weight from one foot to the other, trying to get feeling back into them. She wanted to sit on the cold ground but didn't know if that would be disrespectful, so she stood.

She bumped into Trades with Horses. Her face flushed. She'd fallen asleep standing up. Acknowledging her for the first time in hours, he picked her up and started back toward camp.

Aware of the gazes that followed their progress, she said, "Put me down. I'm fine." She didn't want to appear weak, especially in front of the woman who'd claim him as her own.

Ignoring her request, he carried her back to his sister's teepee without uttering a word. Julia bit her lip to keep silent. She would not ask about this other woman. She did not want him to think that she cared.

The teepee was empty. Both his sister and her husband were still out by the platform with his father's remains. After placing her on her sleeping mat, he stoked the fire, taking the chill out of the small space.

When he knelt by her pallet, she touched his face. His looked tired. There were dark circles around his eyes. She wanted to draw him down beside her, to tell him to rest, but she didn't. "I'm fine. Go back. Your mother and sister need you."

He filled his lungs with a deep breath and bowed his head. She stroked the silky black hair, pushing the fallen strands behind his ears. Her hand trailed from his face to his shoulders where she rubbed at the knotted muscles that bunched beneath his shirt. Tonight he wore a white ceremonial deerskin shirt, something she'd never seen before.

She should be glad he had someone who would be with him after she left. She should just take what he offered now and let that be enough. There could be no lifetime with this man. Only now.

She touched his face again, a deep ache throbbing in her core. She wanted to take his pain away, take it into her body. She ran a hand over his forehead, down his slightly hooked nose, across his full lips. He stiffened at the contact. Strange, she'd never seen Indians kiss their mates. Didn't they kiss? Or did they do it only in their teepees?

Well, no one was around now. She lifted her face to his. After one long moment, she opened one eye. He watched her with a deep frown on his broad forehead.

"Kiss me." She couldn't stop the heat that rose up her neck into her face. Maybe he didn't want to kiss her.

"Kiss?"

"When a man and woman's lips meet."

"I have seen the white man touch his mouth to his woman."

"Haven't you ever wanted to try it?"

He shook his head. "No."

Her heart twisted with disappointment. At first the idea of the kiss was meant to bring him comfort, now she needed his comfort. She wanted to know how his mouth felt against hers.

She placed a hand behind his neck and pulled him down to her level. His breath fanned her cheeks. He pulled back, but now that the thought had taken hold, she had to know his taste. She rose on one elbow and slowly moved closer to his mouth.

Her heart thundered in her ears. Worried he'd push her away, she moved slowly closer and closer to him until her mouth touched his.

His lips were firm but surprisingly soft. Craving more, she pressed her mouth harder to his. She could feel the tension in his body. Did he like it? She drew back to stare up at him. Other than breathing a little faster, he appeared unmoved.

She flushed with shame. How could she have been so forward? Moving away from him, she settled onto her mat, face turned away from his.

To her surprise he didn't leave, but curved his body around hers, and pulled her into his warmth. Something hard pressed into her buttocks. She stiffened and then forced herself to relax. She smiled. The kiss had definitely affected him.

Sunkawakan Iyopeya lay with Julia long after she'd fallen asleep and his sister and her husband had returned.

They moved quietly around the teepee, the silence only broken by his sister's weeping.

No decision would be made in the selection of a new chief until the spring when all members of his tribe would be together. Until that time the few elders of the council and Matosapa would make any necessary decisions.

What chance did he have to be chief without the medicine man's help? Probably none. But give up Julia? He would rather tear out his heart.

Maybe he was being arrogant to believe he was the best choice to lead his people. There were other skilled and courageous warriors, but none had had the vision of the white man's betrayal. If only he could become chief without the help of the medicine man.

He pulled Julia closer. As he did, she mumbled something in her sleep. Was she dreaming of this Vincent? His stomach clenched. He would not share her body or her thoughts with any other, nor would he share his body or thoughts with any other woman. No, he would have only one wife and it would be this one who slept in his arms. He would tell Matosapa of his decision in the morning.

CHAPTER ELEVEN

Early the next morning, Sunkawakan Iyopeya went in search of Matosapa. As he walked through the village toward the medicine man's teepee, he was greeted warmly by tribal members, expressing their admiration of his father and their grief.

"Sunkawakan Iyopeya," a familiar voice call.

Chaske, the medicine man's eldest son, stood outside his mother's teepee.

Sunkawakan Iyopeya touched his oldest friend's shoulder in greeting when they came abreast of each other. Chaske bore his mother's features and his father's height. Sunkawakan Iyopeya eyes were level with his childhood friend. The first smile in many days spread across his face.

"How are you, my brother?" The medicine man's son asked, concern tightening his features.

Before the young man could give voice to more words of grieve and sadness, Sunkawakan Iyopeya spoke first. "You are looking well, but I do not understand why you still share your mother's teepee."

This brought a smile to his friend's face. "For the same reason you do. No woman will have me."

They both shared laughter that seemed so out of place in the silence of the camp. Sunkawakan Iyopeya lost his smile first.

Chaske touched his shoulder in support but did not say anything more.

"I'm looking for your father," Sunkawakan Iyopeya said. "Have you seen him?"

"Possibly down by the river."

Sunkawakan Iyopeya grasped his friend's shoulder with a hard grip, before turning toward his mother's teepee. Better to see her while the day was young and his patience was strong.

The spirit of his father still resided inside the teepee. For Sunkawakan Iyopeya, his father still lived. Still walked the hills, bow in hand, still hunted the buffalo. That he would not see this great hunter again brought more sorrow to his heart than a warrior could admit.

He was saved from entering the teepee by his mother stepping out.

"Good morning, Mother."

She didn't answer but stared over the plain toward the site where his father's body lay. Before her mind could drift away, he gently turned her face so he could look into her eyes. "The medicine man? Have you seen him?"

She shook her head. Her eyes became sharp and direct. More like the woman he knew.

"We must burn this place." She pointed at her teepee.

He swallowed back his protest. It was customary to burn the lodgings of the departed to set their spirit free. "You should build another teepee before you burn this one." Maybe he could delay the torching as long as possible.

She shook her head, the motion sending her grey braids swinging around her narrow shoulders. "I will live with your sister until we can build another shelter."

The mention of his sister brought Julia to mind. "Come. There is someone you should meet."

When he gripped her arm to lead her to his sister's teepee, she jerked away. "I have heard you dishonor us by bringing a woman not of the people to our camp."

Startled, he could only stare at her. "Dishonor? How do I dishonor this family? This is the woman of my heart."

His mother spat on the frozen ground. "The heart. That is white man's talk. The medicine man's daughter is one of the people. She is the woman your father and I chose for you. Would you dishonor your father's wishes?"

An arrow of pain pierced his spirit. His father had been a man of strong character. He was able to see past the hot wind of another's speech right to the heart of the matter. That his father had chosen the medicine's daughter to be his woman made Sunkawakan Iyopeya falter, but only for a moment. He father had also been a generous man. One who allowed others to prove their worth before passing judgment—something his mother was incapable of doing.

"She *is* as one of the people. She is brave, hardworking and fierce of spirit. She will give you many grandchildren."

His mother drew back from him as though he'd struck her. "I do not want children that are not of the people. Save your seed for the medicine man's daughter."

"Mother—"

She held up her hand. "We will speak no more of this. I will burn this teepee when the sun rises again and sleep in your sister's lodge. But only after you remove that woman." Turning on her moccasin-clad feet, she stomped away, heading for the platform where his father's earthly remains lay.

His anger choked him, locking his words deep in his chest. If his father were alive no guest would be treated with such disrespect. But he wasn't. And Sunkawakan Iyopeya had to protect Julia from his mother's hurtful tongue.

It was midday. Julia and Trades with Horses were a little distance from the other teepees. As long as the wind was still, the day was almost pleasant.

"I met one of the women yesterday. Down by the creek." Julia cast a glance at him from beneath her lashes.

Muscles rippled beneath his buckskin shirt as he cleared rocks and dead grass from a large section of land on the outskirts of the camp. Sweat dotted his bronze face. How could he sweat when it was so cold?

"Did she greet you?"

Julia thought about the purple bruise on her arm. "Not exactly."

He studied her for a long moment. *Had she given something away in the tone of her voice?* She glanced down not wanting to meet his gaze, moving pebbles with the toe of her deerskin shoe. She'd decided not to tell him about what had happened down by the creek.

She was hurt knowing he had another woman. But she would not ask him about her.

He gathered many poles together, each longer than his body. "Now that my father is dead, we have to select a new chief."

"Who will it be?" She held her breath. She remembered their talk days earlier. Even though he'd not said so, she knew he wanted to be chief.

Holding the poles together with his left hand, he looped rope around the top end with his right. "Whoever is chosen will be selected in the spring when all the tribe is together."

By spring, she'd be gone.

His black hair blew around his face. Reaching out, she almost swept it off his cheek. She tucked her hand behind her to keep from touching him.

"Who will decide?"

"The medicine man and some of the elders."

She didn't know the elders, but she'd seen the medicine man from a distance. How did he feel about Trades with Horses?

Rising from his knees, he gathered the poles and pushed them into the opening of the buffalo skins they'd sewed together earlier that morning.

"Does he want you to be chief?"

Trades with Horses' mouth tightened to a thin line. "His vote comes with demands." He held up a hand. "We waste time. Our lodging must be up before the sun sets."

"Why do we hurry? Has your sister pushed us out of her teepee?" She smiled to show him she was funnin', but unease stirred in her gut. His sister had not been friendly. She'd said only a few words to Julia in the two days she'd slept in her teepee. Julia didn't have to be hit over the head with a stick to know she wasn't welcome. But she didn't want Trades with Horses to know how uncomfortable she felt. He had too much on his mind with his father's death.

"Our custom is to burn the teepee of the dead." He took a deep breath, his gaze wondering across the field to the spot where his father's body lay. "My mother will live with my sister—her only daughter. There is not enough room for all of us to stay there together." He pointed to the poles and skins. "So that is why I build this shelter for us." He smiled at her. "Unless you like sleeping outside."

Julia saw the pain through his smile. She wanted to hold him but didn't go to him. It wouldn't do for her to let him get close to her heart.

"Well, let's get going." She rubbed her cold hands together to warm them and then helped him drag the poles and skins to the circle he'd created. He shoved the poles upward, and she grabbed one of the long sticks and pulled it out from the bunch.

"Building a teepee is women's work," he said.

He spoke the truth. In the other villages she'd lived **in,** women had built and torn down the teepees when it was time to move. Standing on the opposite side of the circle from her, he pulled another pole from the bunch.

"And what is the work of the men of the tribe?" She wanted him to talk to take his mind off the problems her being in the village had caused. She might not have book learning, but she knew his mother and sister didn't like her.

"To hunt and protect the women and children."

They worked around the circle, pulling the poles from the center until all the sticks were stretched out to their limit.

"I will hunt after we finish."

She almost laughed. He took everything so seriously. Somehow she had to make some good come from being in this camp.

"We could build this teepee for your mother. Your sister and her husband will have children one day. Their tent will be too small. But if you give her this one, you and me could stay here also. It's too big for the two of us." And when she left, he'd have his mother for company.

He studied the poles they'd arranged in a perfect circle. "I will think on your suggestion. But for now we have a few more hours 'til sundown to finish this teepee."

He pulled the buffalo skins all the way down the frame, punched holes in the bottom of the skins, and staked them to the ground. He did this all around the teepee until the poles were invisible from the outside.

When he finished, he tossed the remaining skins to her. "I must hunt." He was gone before she could ask when he'd return.

After she built a fire in the pit to warm the space, she lined the inside of the teepee with the remaining skins to keep out the cold wind. She found peace in the work as the afternoon bleed into early evening.

"Julia."

At the sound of her name, she leapt up from her place beside the fire and opened the flap of the tent. Trades with Horses stood bathed in the reddish glow of the setting sun, his face in shadow. A dead deer was draped over his shoulders.

"Come." He turned and walked away.

She rushed back inside, grabbed her blanket and hastened to catch up to his long stride.

In the center of the camp, he dropped the deer from his shoulders and gave a shout. Heads popped out of their teepees.

The women, Julia included, quickly skinned the animal and cut the meat into chunks. Those not involved in skinning built massive fires. Soon the meat roasted over the flames.

Trades with Horses' mother was absent from the gathering. Julia wondered if this was the time to go and sit with the old lady. But what could she say to his mother? Nothing.

When the food was ready, Trades with Horses personally escorted his mother out of her daughter's teepee and seated her in the place of honor. Julia cut a generous portion of the meat and placed it on a large corn cake. Bowing her head in a show of respect, she offered the food to his mother. For a long moment, Julia thought the old woman would refuse, but Trades with Horses said something sharp and quick to his mother and she took the food.

He gripped Julia by the arm and made her straighten from her stooped position. Raising his voice to be heard over the crowd, he spoke in the language of the people. She only understood one or two words, but he looked at her as he spoke. The gazes of everyone present rested on her.

She swallowed, her throat suddenly dry. She wanted to creep away from all the eyes, but the proud tone of his voice kept her rooted to his side.

Whatever he had said to his mother had not made the old woman happy.

He pointed in the direction of their new teepee and then pointed at his mother. Almost as one, the crowd made an excited noise, and Julia knew he'd used her suggestion of giving the dwelling to his mother. Julia cut her eyes toward the old woman. She wasn't as pleased by the gift as the rest of the tribe.

Julia searched the gathering, looking for Trades with Horses' sister. What would she think of the gift? Julia found her. She stood with her arm around the shoulders of the woman who'd grabbed Julia by the creek. Both were staring at her with a look of hatred in their gazes.

Julia's gut twisted, and she lost her desire for the food.

After his speech, she leaned close to him and whispered in his ear. "Who is the woman standing next to your sister?" She needed to know. She'd only have peace if she knew. Studying his face for a change in expression, Julia didn't breathe as she waited.

"That is Zintkawin, the medicine man's daughter."

Cold fingers tightened around Julia's heart and squeezed. *"His vote comes with demands."* She remembered Trades with Horses' words about the medicine man. Was this why his mother and sister didn't welcome her into their teepee? Did they want this—this Zintkawin to be his woman? Was taking his daughter to wife one of the demands the medicine man made of Trades with Horses? Did Julia stand in the way of his becoming chief?

You'll be up North. What does it matter?

Her mind said go. Her heart said stay.

The night dragged on. Her brain hurt from all the thinking. She wanted to escape to their new home. She wanted to feel the warmth of Trades with Horses' body curled around her.

Her legs fell asleep a little before her head jerked. When his mother left the gathering Julia felt free to seek her bed. Touching Trades with Horses' shoulder, she pointed toward their teepee.

He nodded with understanding.

Rising from her place by his side, she left the cerebration and made her way toward their home.

Away from the bright light of the campfires, the path was dark. She stumbled over the rise and fall of the ground, stubbing her toes. Slowing her pace, she took each step carefully, not wanting to skin her hands and knees.

Grateful Trades with Horses had left the fires burning in their teepee, she used the light to guide her.

A hand clamped over her mouth. She tried to scream. Something sharp and wicked pressed against her neck. A knife. She couldn't stop the whimper that escaped her throat—a throat raw with fear.

Something rattled as her attacker moved to pull her even closer and deeper into the shadows. The breath in her ear was ragged, the strong hand and fingers clamped over her mouth dug into the skin. She didn't move, didn't dare breath.

She'd never reach the North. Never get enough learning to start a school.

She was gonna die.

CHAPTER TWELVE

Just as suddenly she was free, falling to her knees as her attacker fled.

Heart hammering in her chest, she took one breath and then another.

"Julia." Trades with Horses was on his haunches beside her. He gripped her arms, pulling her up. "What happened?" His worried gaze traveled over her face.

She couldn't tell him she'd been attacked. She was an outsider. No one would believe her. Being the honorable man that he was, he'd want to question every person in camp. The tribe would turn against him. He'd never be chief. No, she'd have to keep what happened a secret.

"I fell. Tripped over a root." Because she was such a miserable liar, she couldn't look him in the eye. She pushed out of his arms and walked as fast as her trembling legs could carry her toward the safety of their teepee.

Once inside, she kept to the shadows as she prepared for bed. The spot on her neck ached. When she touched it, her finger came away with a dot of blood. She tried to lift the deerskin dress over her head. Her arms trembled so much she gave up and dropped down on the pallet. She'd sleep in the clothes she'd worn all day.

When Trades with Horses slipped under the skins, she didn't protest. Instead of presenting her back to him as she done on the previous night, she turned into his arms. She needed his comfort.

He stroked her back until her trembling stopped.

"My mother will grow used to you."

Julia didn't say anything. Let him think his mother was the reason she shook in his arms.

Because she'd almost lost her life, she needed his passion, his fire. Pressing her body into his, she felt the moment when he realized what she wanted from him.

He removed her dress in one swift movement. His hands stroked the tender skin of her breast then rubbed a finger across a nipple. She bit her lip to keep from moaning. But when he pinched the swollen nub between his calloused fingers, the moan escaped and floated on the air.

She tugged at his shirt. Pulling it over his head, she tossed it on the ground. His chest was hairless and smooth with corded muscle. She ran her hands over his body like a blind woman learning through feel.

Aware that he muttered words in her ear, she didn't ask him what he'd said. She needed to touch him, to feel his warmth, to feel his heart beat under her palms. He was beautiful, slender but strong. She buried her nose in his neck, loving his scent.

When he settled between her thighs, cold reason washed over her. No one had touched her inner core but Vincent. And he hadn't touched her since before the whipping. Her fire died a sudden death. She tried to close her thighs.

Trades with Horses stared down at her. She stared up at him, trying to tell him with her eyes what she couldn't with her lips. Instead of rolling off, he leaned forward capturing her face between the palms of his hand. Very slowly, he lowered his face to hers, until his breath fanned her skin. With the lightest of touches, he pressed his lips to hers.

Her body went rigid with surprise, and then her eyes drifted closed. The pressure of his mouth increased, stoking the fire in her core. With each pass of his mouth over hers, her legs weakened until they opened completely for him. He loosened his breech cloth. The length of his manhood pressed against her stomach. He continued making love to her mouth, until she reached between them and guided him into her core.

It had been a long time, and at first her body resisted the push of his, but when he touched his tongue to her lips all resistance slipped away. Buried within her, Trades with Horses worshipped her with his body.

She rode a boat on the Great River, holding onto him with each wave of the current, with each stroke of his manhood. Her skin was on fire. Her core vibrated and grew tighter with each plunge of his hips. Her hands ran over his backside, leading him, urging him. Where, she didn't know.

"Hurry," she gasped, just before lights exploded behind her closed lids.

The wind howled, shaking the teepee. Despite the cold outside, Julia lay warm and content within Trades with Horses' embrace. His breath, steady and deep, fanned the back of her neck.

It would be hard to leave in the spring. She'd come to enjoy being with him. He was a man of strength and honor. Unlike Vincent.

Having gone into a dark place, her thoughts naturally turned to the attack. What would Trades with Horses do if she told him she'd been held at knifepoint? She touched the small cut at the base of her throat. Why did someone want to hurt her? She'd asked herself this all night.

How could she protect herself? It would be hard to guard against everyone in the village.

"You do not sleep." His rough voice startled her. He caressed her bare hip and thigh. She settled deeper into his warmth, sighing as the wind rattled outside the teepee. He stroked her body until her eyes closed. She floated in a dreamlike state, aware of his body and voice while reaching toward the peace of sleep.

"Tomorrow we burn my mother's teepee."

All thought of sleep disappeared. His mother would be living with them. Even though, Julia had been the one to suggest she stay in their teepee, the thought of losing this new found peace with Trades with Horses made her sad.

"Why?"

"It allows the spirit of the dead to leave this existence and move on to the next." His arm banded around her middle and pulled her closer.

Even though they'd made love, she didn't know this man, and with the short time they had left, she would never get to know him better. Her heart was torn. On one hand she wanted to be free, on the other she wanted to stay here and grow old with him. But even if she stayed, happiness with him would not come easy. "Your mother does not like me."

He was silent for a moment. "My mother is a difficult woman. She forgets I am a man and can decide my own fate."

Julia thought on those words, trying to understand what he wasn't saying. "What does she want from you?"

He took so long to answer she thought he wouldn't.

"She wants me to marry someone in the tribe."

Her heart pounded so hard she feared he would hear it. She searched the shadows of the teepee as though she could find answers in the drifting grays of the lodging. Why was her body feeling this way when she would leave in the spring? She turned slowly onto her back and stared up at the hole in the teepee, watching the smoke from their fire escape into the night sky.

"Who does she want you to marry?" The calmness in her voice surprised her.

"Zintkawin."

Dark eyes shot full of hatred filled Julia's mind. The medicine man's daughter. Could it have been her who held a knife to Julia's throat? No. This person had been taller. Julia's head rested against her attacker's breastbone. Most definitely a man. Not the short woman who'd she'd met down by the river.

"Does the medicine man want you to marry his daughter?" If he thought Trades with Horses should be the next chief, maybe he also thought like Trades with Horses' mother—the wife of the new chief should be Indian.

"Yes."

"Do you...do you want this woman?"

"She was a childhood playmate...not the woman of my heart. You have my heart."

Julia let out a breath. She turned to face him, no longer afraid to let him see the love shining in her eyes. He gathered her in his arms, and she rested her head on his shoulder. Even as her mind shouted, *No*, her heart said, *yes*, this is where I belong. With this man.

Snowflakes drifted down from the night sky to meet the fire sparks that escaped the burning teepee.

Julia stood at a safe distance from the blaze and watched the medicine man dance as he aided the spirits on their journey.

Earlier in the day as she and Trades with Horses ate their last meal alone, he'd told her what to expect at the burning ceremony.

Now he stood quietly at her side with the light from the flames making shadows on his square face. He wasn't as lost in his grief as he'd been two days ago at his father's burial ceremony, but sadness lingered in his eyes. Wanting to give him comfort as much as needing his warmth, Julia moved closer to him, just touching him with her body.

They'd made love again this morning before dawn had lightened the skies. He'd taken her rougher this time, as though, he could outrun the dark clouds in his future. Gripping him tighter to her body she'd allowed him to lose himself in the heat of their lovemaking. Instead of being frightened by his fierceness, she'd gloried in it, finding a completeness she'd never found with Vincent.

After the ceremony and while the flames smoldered, Julia and Trades with Horses moved his mother's belongings from his sister's teepee to theirs. Later the three of them shared a silent meal of roasted rabbit and root vegetables, all lost in their own thoughts. Without a word, his mother retired to her pallet on the opposite side of the teepee from their sleeping mat.

Trades with Horses rose. "Going to check on the horses."

A current of cold wind entered the teepee as he left. Too cold and too afraid to take a walk outside, Julia sat before the fire, knowing his mother pretended to sleep. It would be a long winter.

When Trades with Horses returned he touched her shoulder and nodded toward their sleeping mat. Julia's eyes strayed to his mother's unmoving form under her furs.

Once under their own furs, he drew her into his body. He stroked her arm, her hip, before trailing his callous fingers down to her thigh. She lay as stiff as a frozen shift on a mulberry bush.

"What is wrong?"

"Your mother," she whispered.

He rose onto one elbow. Frowning, he stared down into her face. "What about my mother?"

"She'll hear."

He glanced beyond the banked fire. "She sleeps."

Julia closed her eyes, doubting his words. The old woman had ears like a hawk. Even now, Julia could detect the change in her breathing.

He resumed his caresses. She hadn't removed her clothes, too ashamed to do so within his mother's sight. He pushed her dress up to her waist and began to stroke her inner thighs. As much as she wanted to enjoy his touch, she couldn't. Had her mother been aware of Julia sleeping across the shack when she and Master Donnelly—

She shut her mind to that thought.

She'd been the one to suggest moving his mother into their teepee. So until spring, this was her life.

Sighing, she sat up, pulled her dress over her head and gave him her body.

"That one is a witch."

Sunkawakan Iyopeya sat across the fire pit from his mother. The sun had barely peaked above the Black Hills and already he was tired of her evil words. He ran a hand over his face. His mother was using Julia's absence—she had gone to the river—to complain about her. If only he had listened to his gut and left the old one to live with his sister.

"She is a bad spirit that has stolen your senses."

He had taught Julia a word here and there of his people's language since they had left Fort Laramie. With her quick mind, she would soon understand his mother's words. He did not want her hurt by the vicious things his mother spouted.

"You will not speak of her in such a manner. She is my woman. The one chosen to bear your grandchildren, and she cannot steal something I give willingly."

"She is no one." Spit bubbled at the corners of his mother's mouth. "Do you believe you can be chief with her as your wife? Which of the elders will cast their vote for a man who does not honor his own people?"

"If they are not wise enough to see I am the best person to lead the tribe, regardless of which woman I choose, then I do not need to be part of this tribe."

Her jaw snapped shut. As much as she thought she was dishonored by Julia being his chosen, she would be more dishonored if he left. Her place in the tribe would be threatened. She controlled many as the wife of the chief. As mother of the chief, she would still have much respect.

"The medicine man—"

"Matosapa is a truly wise man, but he cannot dictate to me who will share my teepee."

His mother straightened her thin body until she quivered like a sapling in the wind. "The flesh has nothing to do with this. This is about your rightful place as chief."

"No, Mother. This is about power. Yours and Matosapa's—"

Julia stepped into the teepee. Holding her soiled garments close to her chest, her worried gaze sought his.

Had she heard their angry voices?

"Morning." She spoke to his mother who sat sullenly before the fire and did not return the greeting.

A deep rose bloomed on Julia's cheeks.

Sunkawakan Iyopeya narrowed his eyes at his mother. "You will speak."

His mother returned the greeting, but her tone was as sour and sharp as an unripe persimmon.

Julia's shoulders tensed. Even though his mother's part of the teepee was in shadow, Julia gaze lingered there. Finally she turned, gave him a fleeting glance and fled outside into the cold.

He followed.

She stood a short distance away from their teepee, staring at the hills. Walking up behind her, he placed his hands on her shoulders, drawing her back into his body. She trembled like a baby bird. He drew her closer, pressing his lips to her ear. "She is an old woman. A woman who has lost her husband and her position in the tribe. She means you no harm." He wished he could believe the words he whispered in his love's hair.

Julia turned and stared up at him, brown eyes liquid with unshed tears. His stomach clenched. Her tears were like arrows piercing his flesh.

"I love you." The white man's words were foreign, but he meant them with all his soul. This woman would be in his heart long after their bodies turned to dust.

CHAPTER THIRTEEN

"There are at least two more months of snow," Chaske said.

Rather than look in the other man's eyes and see the bleak expression he knew would be there, Sunkawakan Iyopeya stared across the great field as the sun's watery rays sank down over the hills. Tomorrow it would snow again. He could smell the wetness in the air.

He and Chaske had caught three rabbits, two prairie dogs and a couple of grouse. Not nearly enough to feed thirty men, women and children. It was as if the elk and buffalo had gone into hibernation with the bear and snake.

"Tomorrow if we start the hunt before the dawn, we might have a bigger bounty." Chaske's words rang hollow.

The weight of the remaining winter months pressed heavily on Sunkawakan Iyopeya's shoulders. Some of his people would not make it to the end of the cold months. They had buried two children in the last week. The clan mothers were sacrificing their food for the children. The dogs in the village had started to disappear.

As he had predicted the wagon of provisions from the Great Father had not made its way to their winter camp. Should he go back to Fort Laramie to beg for food? The skin on his neck tightened and his blood heated at the thought. He could live off roots and berries and the occasional rabbit first. But he had others to care for. There were women and children in the camp.

"I must go to the Fort."

"And if there are still no provisions?" Chaske asked.

Sunkawakan Iyopeya had no answer. What would they do? Move the camp? He shook his head at the thought. They had a plenty of water from the stream, cover from most of the wind and nice flat land for their teepees. It would be foolish to uproot the whole camp. What if they were caught in a squall?

"I will go back to the Fort and plead for sacks of corn and barrels of dried fish."

"And do you think the whites will care about a few dying Indians?" Chaske asked. His words were as bitter as the chokecherries that grew by the river.

He knew the truth of his best friend's words. "I *will* bring back food for my people or die trying."

A wordless exchange passed between them—an unspoken acknowledgement of the perils of going to Fort Laramie.

"You will need someone at your back."

Sunkawakan Iyopeya studied his friend. "We leave in the morning."

Smoke from the cooking fire filled the teepee. Julia had cooked outside until the last day or two, but now the cold drove her inside.

She chopped up the rabbit carcass—their share of the day's hunt—and threw it into a clay cooking pot. Trades with Horses placed a bedroll and a quiver of arrows by the teepee's opening, before taking a seat next to her around the fire.

"Are you going far?" The words burst from her throat. She'd asked in her language, so his mother wouldn't understand. The old woman sat as far away from Julia as she could and still be warm.

Julia didn't like him gone after the sun set behind the hills. Since the attack, she'd never left the teepee alone after dark. She spent her mornings helping the medicine man gather plants for healing. The afternoons were spent down at the creek with the women as they washed their clothes.

His attention stayed on the fire.

As she waited for his answer, her nerves stretched and vibrated like an arrow ready to be released from a bow.

"I will travel to Fort Laramie tomorrow for supplies."

She couldn't draw enough air into her body. Would he take her with him? Before she could ask, his mother barked words into the silence.

The old woman didn't like them to speak in Julia's tongue. But it was fine for her and Trades with Horses to leave Julia out of conversations by speaking in the language of the people.

He answered his mother. Her face paled, but his words silenced her.

Julia glanced between mother and son. She'd only understood the word food and dying. When he and the men returned with small game instead of buffalo and deer or elk, she'd seen the worry on his face. She'd also seen how thin the people had become.

"Can't the hunters travel further for meat?"

"No. Not and return in the same day." He stirred the fire.

The silence pressed down on Julia's heart. Fear made her selfish. "Must *you* go to the Fort?

These words brought his head up sharply. His gaze held Julia's until she could feel the heat in her cheeks—heat that had nothing to do with the fire.

"If my father were alive, he would go. Now it must be Sunkawakan Iyopeya." He pointed to his chest.

But you're not chief. She wanted to say these words but held her tongue.

"The tribe is starving. We will not make it to the spring. Too many will die. Too many have already died." The last he said in a quiet voice.

The despair in his tone sent cold, creeping fingers of fear up her spine. He'd become her rock—unshakeable and unmovable. If he believed this could be their fate, Julia had no reason to doubt him. As she accepted his words, determination filled her mind.

"When do we leave?"

His dark gaze bore into hers. "*We* don't. Chaske will go with me. We leave with the dawn."

"You can't leave me here." Her voice rose and disturbed the moment of peace in the teepee.

In her high-pitched voice, his mother demanded to know what they spoke about.

Their voices floated around her in a sea of words and sounds. There was no way he would leave her here to face whatever danger awaited her. And she had no doubt whoever attacked her several weeks ago would try again. This time Trades with Horses would not be here to come to her rescue.

On their second day of travel, Sunkawakan Iyopeya, Chaske and another friend, Wanbli, rode abreast. The Black Hills a smudge on the horizon behind them. The sun was afraid of the day and hid among the clouds. Though the snow had grown thinner as they rode south, Father Winter's breath blew hard from the North. The wind whipped around their heads and under their buffalo skins to steal the warmth from their bodies. The distance to the Fort was still a week away with hard riding.

Sunkawakan Iyopeya's horse whinnied.

"Someone follows," Chaske said.

Sunkawakan Iyopeya did not turn around. He had been aware for most of the day of someone behind them. Whoever trailed was not a tracker. Night would tell whether this person was friend or foe.

"I will kill them." The medicine man's son did not have the patience and cunning of his father.

"Wait until nightfall," Sunkawakan Iyopeya said.

From the scowl on Chaske's face, Sunkawakan Iyopeya knew his command did not please the younger man.

Sunkawakan Iyopeya would not let anything or anyone stand in the way of his bringing food and supplies back to his tribe, but he wanted to shed as little blood as possible.

When the shadows grew long, they made camp near an outcrop of rocks. They fed and watered the horses, then built a fire, but sat outside the light cast by the flames.

They ate and then pretended to prepare for sleep. Chaske stood and without a word strolled toward the tree line.

Wanbli grunted. "Let us hope Chaske leaves something of the unfortunate one to identity."

Chaske acted first and maybe thought later. But there was no one Sunkawakan Iyopeya would rather have at his side in battle.

His horse whinnied—not in unease but almost in welcome. Body tense, Sunkawakan Iyopeya took in the stillness of the night. The richness of the soil, poignant with the moisture from the snows filled his nose along with the subtle scent—

He leapt to his feet.

"What is wrong?" Wanbli asked.

Gut cramping and mouth dry, Sunkawakan Iyopeya raced off in pursuit of Chaske. His footfalls mocked the heavy thud of his heart.

The wind howled around the rocks like the sound of coyotes baying to each other. Julia shivered and wrapped the old buffalo fur tighter around her body as she led Moon Magic to a patch of prairie grass.

"Thank you." She stroked the horse's sides. His warmth took the chill from her cold, stiff fingers.

Cold days and colder nights. She hadn't dared build a fire. Trades with Horses and his companions would have seen her. And to keep from being recognized, she'd worn a pair of his buckskin pants and kept a blanket wrapped around her head.

She was tired of being cold. Her only warmth had come from the buffalo skin she'd wrapped in at night and the heat from Moon Magic's body during the day. Her teeth chattered, she was hungry, and her butt was sore from riding all day without a break. Would she be able to keep up this pace all the way to the fort? She slept fitfully in fear they'd break camp and she not know it.

She'd had no idea what to expect as she followed Trades with Horses to Fort Laramie. But she'd had no choice. She couldn't stay in the winter village.

Last night, she'd almost stumbled into their camp. Her heart thumped wildly in her chest as she'd hid behind boulders with both hands clamped around her mount's muzzle.

Now, she staggered a short ways into the woods to relieve herself before sleeping. As she stepped into the shelter of the trees, the hairs on her neck quivered. Stopping, she scanned the tree line. The moon was hidden behind the clouds and the spaces between the pines seem to dance with danger.

Her need to pee vanished as quickly as her fear had sprung. She backed away from the pitch black of the woods.

A punishing hand clamped over her mouth, and a bruising arm crushed her body into a hard chest.

The hand at her mouth disappeared, and before she could draw breath to scream, something sharp pricked her throat. A trickle of warm, wet liquid ran down her throat. Her blood.

A pungent odor of animal grease filled her nose. Memories of another night flooded her brain. Blackness appeared in her vision. Her heart thundered in her ears. She couldn't think. Couldn't breathe. Couldn't move.

"Please," she whispered, the word barely escaping her stiff lips.

"You die this time." A man's voice. He shifted his body and something rattled. A bear teeth necklace.

Her body froze.

Her attacker.

Her attacker was here. Not back in the winter camp.

She'd left the Indian village running from death only to find it out here on the Plains. And Trades with Horses didn't know she was about to die a short distance from him.

"Please," she pleaded again. Tears leaked from her eyes. She hated herself for this weakness. Why did she cry now? She needed to be strong.

She couldn't catch her breath. Her mother's face appeared to her, then Bo's, and lastly Trades with Horses. Her heart twisted with what was not to be.

"Chaske!"

Her attacker's body stiffened.

The sound of Trades with Horses' voice made her knees collapse in hope.

Without releasing her or dropping the knife at her throat, her attacker turned both their bodies toward Trades with Horse.

"Do you not recognize my woman?" Trades with Horses asked. Even in the near darkness, she could see the fast rise and fall of his shoulders, hear the fear in his voice.

Her attacker jerked her chin up and dug the knife deeper into her flesh.

She bit down on a cry.

Trades with Horses eyes met hers. She didn't look away. If this was to be her last breath, she wanted his face to be the last she saw.

"I recognized her." Her attacker laughed.

The sound made her stomach clench. She fought the desire to loss her water.

"She is not worthy to be your wife. Zinkinwan is your rightful wife. Not this one." Her attacker's arms tightened around her neck until she struggled for breath. "She must die."

"Do not do this, Chaske." Trades with Horses' hand was outstretched toward her attacker. "Zinkinwan is the sister of my heart, but—"

Her attacker's body jerked.

Julia closed her eyes waiting for the knife to slice away her life. The pain didn't come.

Instead his death grip on her neck loosened, and his arm fell away. Without his arm holding her up, Julia's knees crumbled. She sank to the ground. In the moonlight, she saw him swaying above her. She couldn't move. Couldn't understand what was happening. Then he was falling. His body hit the ground with a thud. His eyes stared sightlessly into hers. Something silver—a blade—dug deep into his back.

A third Indian walked out of the shadows.

No. No. No. Julia started crawling backwards, trying to put distance between her and this new enemy.

Strong hands grabbed her. She clawed and scratched at the hands that hooked onto her body.

"Julia," Trades with Horses' voice pierced the fog of fear that surrounded her.

He pulled her into his arms, crushing her to his body. She wasn't sure if the thunderous beating of a heart was hers or his.

She peered around his body. The third Indian knelt at her attacker's side and placed a hand gently on the dead man's shoulder.

Safe in the circle of Trades with Horses' arms, Julia dared look at the body that lay on the ground. Shock coursed through her. Even in the moonlight, she recognized him. She'd seen him once or twice in camp.

Why was this Chaske willing to kill for the medicine man's daughter?

CHAPTER FOURTEEN

Dark clouds scurried across the fading evening sky as Fort Laramie appeared on the horizon. Sunkawakan Iyopeya held up a hand. Wanbli came abreast, but Julia hung back. She had been silent during their four day journey together since they had buried Chaske.

Sunkawakan Iyopeya had pushed them hard to get to the Fort. He had been angry. He was still angry. Angry with Chaske, angry with her, but mostly angry with himself. He had failed her. He was her protector. Why had she not come to him and told him about the attack?

Why had Chaske, a worthy warrior, felt the need to kill a woman? And if he was defending his sister's honor, why hadn't he demanded to fight Sunkawakan Iyopeya like an honorable Sioux?

These questions rolled around in his mind until his head ached. Questions he would never have answers to.

Julia huddled in the skins atop Moon Magic. Her face was tight and cold, her lips dried and cracked.

He had no choice but to bring her to Fort Laramie. He could not spare Wanbli to take her back. The plan would not work without a second person. Because of Chaske's death they would not be able to bring as much food to the other villages.

He was also worried there might be others involved in the plan to kill her. The only safe place was with him.

"Before dawn we will break into the general store, take what is owed our people, and load the provisions on the backs of pack horses, then ride like the wind from the fort." Sunkawakan Iyopeya spoke to Wanbli but was aware of Julia's gaze on his back.

Dangerous? Yes. But he would not go to the white man and beg for food. The chiefs of the white man had promised his people provisions in exchange for the safe passage of the whites across their land. The Sioux and the Cheyenne had upheld their part of the bargain. The white man had not. Now he must take what was rightfully theirs to keep his people from starving. He only hoped the cost would not be too high.

Carved rocks surrounded a small depression in the ground. This would be the best place to wait for darkness. "We will rest until the moon is high in the sky."

He jump off his horse and went to Julia to help her dismount. She pushed his hand away and slid off Moon Magic, stumbling in her tiredness.

"I'll take care of him," he said when she reached for the horse's reins. Without a word or a smile she walked away, her steps heavy on the frozen ground.

The Plains spread out around them, flat and endless. Fires could be seen at night, so they settled in a depression, wrapped their skins around their bodies and waited.

He gathered her in his arms. Wanbli rested a few feet away, his back turned to give them privacy. Privacy they did not need. She had not touched him willingly since Chaske had been killed.

What would happen to her if he were killed? It was too late to think of that now. He would succeed. The Great Spirits would not let him fail. He would bring food back for his people, and he and Julia would live long fruitful lives together. Their children would roam this land for hundreds of the white man's years.

Her soft breaths calmed his spirit. He closed his eyes, but sleep wouldn't come.

The chill woke Julia. She held her breath, listening. Nothing but the moan of the wind and the pounding of her heart. Not even the restless shifting of the horses. Panic settled with gnawing hunger in her chest. Had he left her? Rising on her hands and knees, she crawled out of the hole in the ground.

Her breath left her lungs in a relieved sigh. Trades with Horses had not departed for the Fort. He and Wanbli were mounted. They each held the reins of two packhorses.

She frowned. Cold fingers of unease crept up her spine to overlay her initial relief. A distance away, still hobbled, Moon Magic nibbled at prairie grass.

Her gaze sought Trades with Horses'. Questioning. His answer lay in the hardening of his jaw, the tight grip on his mount.

"Go back to sleep."

Anger flashed up her back like the heat from a branding iron. "Sleep while you get yourself killed? You need me. Your plan would work better with three instead of two. Think how much more supplies we could deliver to the camp. We might have enough to feed another village."

She waited, her breath trapped in her lungs, pain tearing at her heart. He couldn't leave her here. He couldn't.

He'd always been solemn, feelings held in tight, but for the first time she saw his anger directed at her. His eyes were like black pits of coal dust. "You do not belong out there." He pointed in the direction of the distant fort.

She exploded with heat, the edges of her vision catching fire. "You mean because I'm a woman, don't you?"

His lack of answer told her all she needed to know. He thought she was soft.

Julia dropped the buffalo skin that still held the warmth of their combined bodies. Not caring that Wanbli sat silently beside Trades with Horses, she ripped at the ties of her buckskin top, impatient in her anger. She didn't feel the cold, her skin was too hot.

She gave him her back. "See these scars? I know you've felt them." She fired the words over her shoulder like bullets. "Ever wonder how I got them? Well, it weren't from sitting on a porch with a parasol over my head or grinding corn or skinning game."

She was sorry now she hadn't told him about her beating or about the long, cruel hours in the fields.

She pulled the top back over her shoulders. Her nipples had reacted to the cold, even though her neck burned hotter than a blacksmith's forge. "I'm tough. I can help."

Wanbli tugged on the reins of his horse and moved away from them. Beyond pride, she went to Trades with Horses and placed a hand on his leg.

She'd come too far, endured too much. "Please." The word tore out of her chest with burrs attached, bringing her heart up with it.

A heart he crushed. "You will stay."

He pulled on the reins on his horse, turning the mount's head toward the fort. With Wanbli on his heels, Trades with Horses galloped away.

"I won't be here when you come back," she shouted, tears blurring her vision. "I'm heading north."

When the clouds drifted across the moon again, Sunkawakan Iyopeya and Wanbli, riding low on their mounts galloped across the plain. Keeping upwind of the fort's hobbled horses, they led their ponies into the open field to mingle with the soldiers' mounts. A chestnut roan rolled its eyes and shifted restlessly.

"Shh…" Sunkawakan Iyopeya allowed the mare to take in his scent. He placed a hand lightly on her back, stroking from crown to rump, whispering soothing words. The roan's movements stilled and its breathing slowed.

When he felt the horses had accepted their presence, Sunkawakan Iyopeya squatted. Wanbli knelt to his right. They waited patiently to see if anyone stirred in the scattering of buildings that faced the open field.

"Chaske said she had stolen your wits. That she was a she-devil."

Anger burned bright in Sunkawakan Iyopeya's blood. How had he failed to see the hatred Chaske nurtured in his soul? Was it only for Julia? Or had his childhood friend come to hate him because he had not chosen his sister to wed?

"You have seen her these few days. Do you believe she is a spirit?"

Wanbli's laughter did not carry on the wind. "No. She is just a woman. A hot-tempered one but still only a woman."

Sunkawakan Iyopeya glanced sideways at his companion. Wanbli had been his childhood friend, as had Chaske. But somewhere in the years since their Sun Dance ceremony, their paths had gone in separate directions. Wanbli's life consisted of hunting and fighting only. He knew nothing of making a life with a woman—of making a woman happy.

"Are you still my brother?"

He could feel the heaviness of Wanbli's gaze. "I will always be your brother."

"I place Julia's safety in your hands."

Sunkawakan Iyopeya waited. Had their paths taken them too far from each other? Could he trust his most prized possession to this man?

"I will protect your woman," Wanbli said.

Sunkawakan Iyopeya studied Wanbli for a long moment. His friend did not look away but held his gaze, until it was Sunkawakan Iyopeya who turned away.

He nodded. "It is time." He moved swiftly through the grazing horses, staying clear of their shifting hooves and tails.

He had been to Fort Laramie twice. When he was younger, he'd traveled here with his father. The fort had been a fur trading outpost and an adobe wall enclosed the buildings. The soldiers of the Great White Father had taken over the trading center and turned it into a military outpost.

He knew one of the outlying buildings was the big chief's quarters. The long building housed the horse soldiers and the Post Store.

They would load as many sacks of grain and dried meats as four horses could carry. Afterwards, he and Wanbli would make their way back to camp. Hopefully without bloodshed.

The horses grazed about five hundred paces from the out buildings. Two guards patrolled around the buildings. One sentry was positioned at the armory and did not patrol. Sunkawakan Iyopeya watched until he knew how long it took the two to do one rotation. They met half way, turned and marched back in the direction they'd come.

Torches burned at each end of the long barracks, in front of the armory and near the Post store. The light near the store would make finding the provisions easier but would make him and Wanbli more visible.

Sunkawakan Iyopeya and Wanbli sprinted for the shelter of the soldier's sleeping quarters. Keeping to the shadows, they flattened themselves against the wooden structure. Sunkawakan Iyopeya signaled his intent to take the guard that patrolled the northern portion of the fort. Wanbli would take the other guard.

When Sunkawakan was in position to intercept his sentry, he stopped and waited. Picking up a pebble, he tossed it over the head of the guard. The rock hit the ground with a soft plunk. Gun raised, the guard pivoted in the direction of the sound.

He was at the sentry's side before the man could turn around. He caught the soldier around the throat, tightened his hold until the man's body sagged. He dragged the soldier back to the shadows of the building, gagged him and tied his arms and legs together.

He crept back to the Post store. There, he knelt and went to work on the padlock, securing the entrance. Using his knife, he wedged the blade behind the lock's metal plate. He pulled on the knife handle, rending away the screws. They scattered with a hollow ping on the worn planks of the walkway.

Wanbli appeared at his side, breathing rapidly.

They slipped into the store. The scent of cured hides and coffee robbed Sunkawakan Iyopeya's senses. Underneath these smells were tobacco and sweat.

The torch lit the front of the store. The back of the room was black as a gopher's hole.

The moon escaped the clouds. Torchlight and moonlight combined, chasing away the store's shadows. Mounted on the wall across from the door was a demon from the Spirit world. Sunkawakan Iyopeya palmed his knife ready to do battle with the creature. Light shifted until he stared at the hairy muzzle of a buffalo head.

Feeling foolish, he relaxed his grip on the knife and then sheathed it.

He and Wanbli went to work. In a short time they had sacks of grain and salted meat stacked near the door. They had to load the packhorses quickly. The guards could be found soon.

He opened the door just wide enough to peer out. Nothing moved. He slipped through the opening and, crouching low, sprinted for the horses.

Cautiously he separated his horses from the herd and moved them closer to the store. His blood pounded loudly in his ears, making it hard to hear. This had been too easy. He scanned the grounds. Still nothing moved.

They made short work of loading the sacks. Even as a cold wind kicked up dirt, sweat trickled down Sunkawakan Iyopeya's back.

One of the packhorses whinnied.

He and Wanbli paused, waiting, eyes and ears alert. Half the sacks sat near the Post store door, ready to load. If they had to leave them, not all the villages would get grain.

Whispering to the restless horse, Sunkawakan Iyopeya stroked the animal's neck as his gaze scanned the compound. Wanbli continued to load provisions.

"Intruder." A voice rang out in the silent night.

"Go," Sunkawakan Iyopeya commanded.

There were four more sacks. Wanbli made a move to load them.

"No." Sunkawakan Iyopeya gripped the other man's arm. An unspoken exchange passed between them. They had planned for this possibility.

More voices. Louder. Angry.

Wanbli bounded onto his horse. Sunkawakan Iyopeya handed him the reins of the four horses. His friend would leave two of the loaded mounts in the field for Sunkawakan Iyopeya to retrieve later.

Sunkawakan Iyopeya raced toward the Post store. He leapt and gained access to the roof overhang. Pulling himself up and over, he looked down on the grounds. Soldiers milled around like maggots on a buffalo carcass.

Wanbli made it into the pastured horses just as soldiers ran around to that side of the fort.

Sunkawakan Iyopeya focused his attention on a single building on the other side of the grounds. A lantern hung from a hook by the door. One guard paced in front. His head swung back and forth as sounds from the other side of camp reached him. An unseasoned warrior.

Dropping from the roof, Sunkawakan Iyopeya dashed toward the guard, weaving as he ran. The young man raised his weapon and fired. The bullet pierced Sunkawakan Iyopeya's side. A trail of burning fire raced up his body. He kept running. Before the sentry could load again, Sunkawakan Iyopeya was on him. He tore the rifle from the young man's hands. As the soldier opened his mouth to shout, Sunkawakan Iyopeya hit him in the face with the butt of the weapon. The soldier staggered but did not fall. Sunkawakan Iyopeya hit the man again—this time in the head. The soldier dropped heavily like a buffalo felled by many arrows.

Sunkawakan Iyopeya dashed toward the door of the armory and using the stock of the soldier's gun battered the padlock until it shattered in pieces. Blood leaked from his side and flowed like hot steam, soaking his shirt. *Hurry.*

He lifted the lantern from its hook by the door and pitched it into the dark space. Glass cracked. Slowing only long enough to grab the soldier's collar, he dragged the sentry toward the shelter of the soldier's quarters.

Sound expanded in Sunkawakan Iyopeya's head. Time slowed and then rushed past him in a roar of sound. A roar that hurled his body through the air. Pain exploded in his back. Pain in his head. His one thought before blackness claimed him was of Julia.

CHAPTER FIFTEEN

Boom!

The explosion sent a tremor through the earth that vibrated beneath Julia's feet. She clutched Moon Magic's reins as the night sky lit up with fire. The horse's ears flattened against its skull, its eyes widening with each blast.

"Shh..." She tried to calm the animal as she'd seen Trades with Horses do, but her stroking was more to calm herself.

What was happening? Where was he?

Forgotten were the harsh words they'd said to each other when he'd left. She just wanted him safely back here with her. He needed her. She could feel it.

Throwing herself on the back of Moon Magic, she kneed the horse and headed for the fort. She'd happily endure Trades with Horses' anger later.

Gunfire split the night. Her heart hammered in her chest with each boom. As she drew closer, wild, frightened horses raced past.

Out of the chaos, a rider raced toward her.

Her heart lifted in her chest and immediately sank like a boulder in a stream. The rider rode the horse all wrong. The tilt of his head and the shape of his body were all wrong.

Wanbli, not Trades with Horses.

Moon Magic pranced wildly beneath her. She pulled back on the reins and struggled to control the animal as she scanned the horizon for Trades with Horses.

Wanbli shouted over the bedlam. She saw his mouth move but couldn't hear the words. He waved her back. She ignored him, her eyes straining to see through the smoke.

Soldiers raced around the distant grounds like mice with their tails on fire. But still no sign of Trades with Horses.

Wanbli was close enough now she could see his pinched lips.

"Ride, woman," he shouted.

"Where is Trades with Horses?"

"Trades…" He blinked, his face twisted in confusion, and then it cleared. "Sunkawakan Iyopeya is back there." He pointed in the direction of the fort, in the direction of the fire and chaos.

"You left him?" Anger made her head swell and throb. She wanted to leap off her horse and beat him senseless.

Before she could turn Moon Magic's head toward the fort, Wanbli grabbed the horse's reins from her hands.

"Listen, you crazy woman. He set fire to the white man's gun house, so we could get away. Let him meet the Great Spirit with honor."

The meaning of his words whirled in her head until she couldn't draw breath. "Noooo…"

Wanbli slapped Moon Magic's rump and the animal took after the other horses. Her cries of frustration were lost in the passing wind.

The air, cold and biting, stung her face and dried her tears.

She couldn't leave him. She couldn't. But Wanbli and two of the four pack horses hemmed her in on one side and the other two horses enclosed her and Moon Magic on the right. She could only move forward.

Wanbli set a fast pace. The exploding fireworks became a distance sound as the horses hooves pounded across the frozen earth.

Her tears stung her chapped face. Her soul cried out his name. He wasn't dead. He couldn't be. Her heart would know it. But each glance behind her revealed no rider racing to catch up to them.

Wanbli didn't let her rest until they reached the river. It was shallow, and the horses' hooves cracked the ice that covered the water. When they crossed to the other bank, he allowed the horses to drink, and they rested. He offered her dried meat and berries. At the sour smell, she heaved and emptied the contents of her stomach on his moccasins.

A thousand buffalo hammered on Sunkawakan Iyopeya's skull. He tried to open his eyes, but his lids were weighted down. Words, spoken in the white man's tongue, seeped into his mind under the pain.

"How are you feeling, lad?"

The voice was familiar.

"I feared ye were dead. All bloody were ye."

Bloody?

He forced his eyes open. Light pierced his brain like a lance. He lay on a soft pallet, and the white man's shaman—the priest—leaned over him.

He remembered. The fort, the armory explosion.

Julia.

He tried to rise. A pain like the stabbing of a buffalo horn tore through his back and tried to separate his ribs. He gripped the pallet, swallowed and tried to ride out the agony.

"Take it easy." The priest pushed him gently down onto the soft bed.

He needed to get to Julia. "How—"

"Do you remember what happened, lad?"

He remembered. "How long have I been here?" He glanced around the priest's room. The window coverings were drawn tight.

"Two weeks."

"Two weeks...Julia..." Pushing the priest's restraining hands away, Sunkawakan Iyopeya swung his legs over the pallet. The room spun. He gripped his head between his hands to stop the spinning. "I must go."

The priest put a restraining hand on his arm. "You can't leave. The soldiers will kill you if you step outside these rooms. So far they don't know you're here. I've sent my housekeeper away."

He stared up into the faded blue eyes of the old priest. "How—"

The priest's brown, speckled hands clutched the cross at his waist. "You landed practically at my door. I dragged you inside."

He stared at the old man. "Why?" His throat was dry and the word came out a whisper.

The priest—Sunkawakan Iyopeya searched his memory for the old man's name—walked slowly to a table by the bed, picked up a cup and handed it to him. Sunkawakan Iyopeya peered into it. Water. He guzzled it, almost choking in his rush.

"Slow down, son." The priest gently took the empty container and placed it back on the table. "You asked why I help you."

Sunkawakan Iyopeya nodded, immediately regretting the movement.

"I disagree with my people's treatment of the natives. God intended we should live on the land in harmony. Not drive one group of out for the other to profit."

Sunkawakan Iyopeya found it strange a white man would have this belief. Too many did not. The old man would have to be watched to see if his beliefs matched his action.

"The slave woman, is she still with you?" The priest's— Father Keegan was his name—pale blue gaze searched his face.

Why was the old man asking about Julia? He had met her one time and had not spoken more than two words to her.

"She waits for me." Confusion fogged his brain like a spider's web. If he had been here in the priest's rooms for two weeks, she would be back at his village. Did she think him dead? Did everyone think him dead? His stomach twisted when he thought of her pain—of his mother's pain. He had to leave.

His own agony gripped him in its fist and held tight. When the throbbing had faded, he was weak and sweaty.

The priest, unaware of Sunkawakan Iyopeya's misery, stared at the small table by the bed. The table, identical to the one in his parlor, held pictures, pictures of small children, women and men dressed in suits—not priest smocks.

"You killed a guard." The priest's eyes had turned hard and sharp. The fumbling old man was gone.

Confused, Sunkawakan Iyopeya frowned. "I did not kill. I left him tied and bound." He remembered there had been two guards. What had happened to the young one?

The old man studied Sunkawakan Iyopeya through watery eyes. He nodded. "I believe you."

"There was another soldier guarding the armory."

With slow steps, the priest shuffled back toward the small table. "That guard lost an arm." The old man glanced over at him. "He'll live. He's recovering in the fort hospital." The priest gathered up pictures and placed them into a trunk.

For the first time, Sunkawakan Iyopeya noticed that white cloth covered all the furniture in the room.

"The fort's commander, along with the Indian agent, believed the attack to be the work of Indians from the neighboring village. They've sent out patrols. The patrols haven't returned." The old man met Sunkawakan Iyopeya's gaze. "They'll return soon and will start questioning and searching. I will not be immune. Therefore, it's necessary for me to leave."

The priest placed the last of the pictures in the trunk and closed it. "Necessary for *us* to leave."

Sunkawakan Iyopeya struggled from the bed and to his feet. His legs shook, buckled, and he started to fall.

Father Keegan was not as feeble as Sunkawakan Iyopeya thought. The old man's arms wrapped around him, keeping him from falling face first onto the floor.

"I've been thinking about this. It is better that you and I leave together."

Sunkawakan Iyopeya stared down at the pale egg shape of the man's head. "The soldiers might harm you if you are with me."

The old priest chuckled. "Who said anything about them seeing us leave together? As far as they are concerned, I'm just an old man of God finally getting tired of this Godforsaken place."

The old man babbled on. His mouth moved, but no sound came from his lips. The room blackened, and the walls crept toward Sunkawakan Iyopeya. His last conscious thought was the priest had many useless words.

The sun sank low on the horizon as Julia and Wanbli entered the Sioux winter camp ten days later. The village appeared empty except for a dog with its ribs showing beneath sagging skin. It sniffed and pawed the burnt ashes of an old fire.

Julia's legs were as heavy as her spirit as she swung off the back of Moon Magic. She glanced in the direction of the teepee she and Trades with Horses had built. If his mother hated her before, she'd kill her now. Julia had abandoned the old woman's only son to the white soldiers. She leaned her head against Moon Magic's throat. The horse blew warm air into her hair and then butted Julia's head with a wet nose.

She straightened her shoulders and said a brief prayer. Without Trades with Horses she was a lost soul. He'd become so much a part of her that what had been important before had no meaning now. If he had lived, she would have never left this tribe.

Wanbli shouted to let the villagers know they had returned.

People stepped out of their teepees. Julia watched for Trades with Horses' mother, but she didn't appear. His sister and her husband were among the first. Lastly came the medicine man's daughter.

Julia avoided their eyes. Soon enough they'd find out the fate of their brother and...and... She wasn't sure what to call what existed between Trades with Horses and the medicine man's daughter.

"We have food." Julia heard the false hardiness in Wanbli's tone.

A current of excitement swelled through the tribe. Men patted Wanbli on the back and began to unload the sacks from the trail weary horses.

"Where is Sunkawakan Iyopeya?"

Julia shrank within herself. The voice belonged to his sister.

Neither Julia nor Wanbli spoke. Their eyes met briefly. He went back to pulling the sacks off the horses. Did he expect her to tell everyone what had happened?

"Yes, where is my son?"

She flinched but turned to face Trades with Horses' mother. The woman's cold black eyes rested heavily on Julia's face.

Her throat clogged with tears, making it impossible for the words to break free. She opened her mouth, but her heart wouldn't let her say the words.

"He is dead. Killed by the white soldiers," Wanbli said, saving her from speaking. "He has joined the Great Spirit."

The silence was so thick Julia could hear the wind whispering through the trees. A wail ripped through the silence and tore out her heart. Tears blurred her vision. Tears she'd beaten back all through the voyage, when they stopped at the Cheyenne village to gift them a few bags of the provisions, when they approached the camp site where she'd almost lost her life to the medicine man's son, when she and Wanbli had crested the hills and stared down at the winter camp, knowing what would come, these tears now rushed from her eyes like a river overflowing its banks.

Trades with Horses' mother sank to her knees, her hands tearing at her clothes. Julia wanted to go to the old woman, but she knew her attempt to comfort would be rejected.

She stared out over the heads of the people gathered around the horses. The medicine man stood at the edge of the crowd.

"And my son?" his voice rang out over the wails of Trades with Horses' mother.

She and Wanbli had not discussed how they would break the news of Chaske's death. They had been so lost in their own grief this had not occurred to them.

"Chaske was also killed by the white soldiers."

Julia didn't look at Wanbli or at the medicine man. She knew the lie would be on her face for all to see. She was thankful Wanbli hadn't said he had killed his best friend. She was nothing to these people. It would not go well for her if they knew she was the cause of one Sioux killing another.

More wailing filled the air. The combined grief pulled at her spirit. She picked up Moon Magic's reins and pushed through the crowd, heading for the creek. There she sat and stared out over the water as the animal drank his fill.

The birds shared her grief—no squawking and singing. She needed their song to lift her heavy spirit.

The sun's last rays faded from the water's edge. Tomorrow the sun would rise. But Trades with Horses' would never walk this earth again. She placed a hand over her stomach. He would never see his child's face.

Sunkawakan Iyopeya leaned weakly against the door that led out of the priest's rooms onto the Fort's grounds.

Grounds he had not seen in over two weeks. He listened for the creak of the wheels signaling Father Keegan's arrival with the wagon.

He would climb into the buckboard—a questionable feat—lie down in the back, cover himself with blankets, and wait for the priest to place trunks on top of him. He cringed. If the old man were lucky enough to get the trunks up, he would probably drop them on Sunkawakan Iyopeya's already injured head.

Two guards would accompany the old priest to the boat that would take him to Saint Louie. Sunkawakan Iyopeya would stay hidden in the wagon and leave sometime during the first night.

"No killing," the priest had stated when he'd informed Sunkawakan Iyopeya about the guards. "I will not be a part of any killing." He held Sunkawakan Iyopeya's gaze until he nodded.

The old man's mouth twisted into an expression part mirth and part pain. "I will not have you swear on the *Bible*, you being a heathen and such. But your word will suffice."

Now as he waited inside the old priest's quarters, sweat dotted his face and made his clothes—white man's clothes—stick to his body. Several bullets had found their mark in his shoulder and back. And his head still ached with each throb of his heart.

The creak of wheels sounded. He opened the door just wide enough to peer out. Cool air brushed his face. He breathed deeply of the fresh air, the first he had felt and smelled since he had been injured.

The old man motioned for him to hurry. Dawn would arrive soon and soldiers would come to load the priest's possessions into the wagon.

He reached beside the door for the wooden leaning stick he'd carved to help him to the wagon.

"Are you leaving, Father?" Out of nowhere, a soldier had appeared at the priest's side.

Heart doing a war dance in his chest, Sunkawakan Iyopeya had one glimpse of the old man's white startled face before he slowly closed the door. He leaned his forehead against the frame. What if the guard came into the priest's quarters? He would be forced to kill the soldier.

No. The crafty old man would think of something.

He strained to hear the two men's conversation through the heavy oak door.

Father Keegan laughed. "I thought I could help the soldiers by loading some of my smaller items onto the wagon. A man likes to think he's not completely helpless, no matter what his age."

The soldier said something Sunkawakan Iyopeya could not hear. But there were no footsteps on the boards that led to the priest's rooms.

"Thank you." The priest's voice seemed loud. "I'll wait. Thank you again."

Leaning heavily on his makeshift cane, Sunkawakan Iyopeya moved back, allowing the old man to enter. White as the bed sheets, the old priest leaned heavily against the doorframe once it was closed behind him. His gaze sought Sunkawakan Iyopeya's.

Then his mouth wobbled as he attempted a smile. "Close." He closed his eyes, his pale, brown speckled hands clutching the material of his smock at his chest. "Very close." His hands sought his beads. "We will have to wait."

Sunkawakan Iyopeya, whose own breath was returning to normal, bit back a harsh reply. He tired of waiting. He needed to leave. Already the winds had turned slightly warmer. By the time he made his way back across the plains, spring would be on his heels. His tribe might be gone from the winter camp.

He bit back his impatience. "We will wait."

Hobbling back to one of the chairs, he dropped heavily into it. The priest worked the beads, and Sunkawakan Iyopeya worked the head of the wooden cane.

They waited.

CHAPTER SIXTEEN

A week after returning from Fort Laramie, Julia waited at the creek for the medicine man. The sun was sinking over the hills. Most of the tribe would be busy with their preparations for dinner, so she could speak to him with no one the wiser.

The scent of roasting meat drifted from the camp. Instead of making her hungry, the smell of the food made her stomach flip and her mouth filled with water that tasted like copper. She turned her head and spat.

She would miss this beautiful land. Already the prairie wild flowers had started to push out of the soil. Soon, according to what Trades with Horses had told her, yellow and orange blossoms would appear. They would open and close with the rise and set of the sun.

Already she'd stayed too long. If she didn't leave now, she would deliver the babe before she completed her journey to Canada.

"Speak," the medicine man commanded.

She jumped. Her heart pounded in her throat like the drums from the previous evening. He'd crept up on her without her being aware. Or maybe she'd been too lost in her thoughts.

Taking a deep breath and closing her mind to Trades with Horses' face, she said, "I will leave this place, but I need your help."

His lips quivered, the only reaction to her news. Julia bit down on her anger. Even with Trades with Horses dead, his mother and this man had wanted Julia gone from the village. Trades with Horses' mother had moved back to her daughter's teepee, leaving Julia to occupy the lodging alone.

She tried not to be bitter. His mother had lost a husband and a son in a short time. The village had lost someone who would have made a great chief. She'd lost the love of a wonderful man. If he'd returned with her from the fort, she would not have left his side. It was sad she'd only realized the value of what she had after it was gone.

"I will need a horse, some food, and a guide."

The medicine man nodded. "I will make it so."

The stomach sickness struck again. She swallowed repeatedly to keep from disgracing herself. He didn't need to know about the baby nor did Trades with Horses' mother. Not that they would beg her to stay if they knew. Neither one would be happy with a half-breed child in their camp.

"When the sun rises?" he asked.

"Yes," she whispered, her voice clogged with unshed tears. She hadn't planned to leave quite so soon, but leaving tomorrow would be better than two or three weeks from now.

His black eyes held hers for a long moment, before he turned and walked away into the growing darkness.

He knew about the babe. She could feel the certainty in her bones.

Julia and Wanbli plodded along the base of the Black Hills, the wind, blowing steadily at their backs held a hint of warmth. They'd only been on the journey a short time. The medicine man had appeared at her teepee with Moon Magic, food, and Wanbli earlier that morning.

The steady clip clop of the horses' hooves made her sick instead of sleepy. Her stomach twisted and heaved. She kneed Moon Magic into the woods, leaned over and threw up her breakfast. Her horse fidgeted, throwing a wild-eyed glance over its shoulder at her.

"Sorry, boy," she croaked. She rinsed her mouth with the water pouch. After a moment, her stomach settled, and she hurried to catch up with Wanbli.

A tight band of fear squeezed her chest as she thought about the long journey ahead. Would she make it to Canada before she became too big with child?

The medicine man had told her of friendly Sioux tribes where she might find shelter. But what would happen when she left Sioux territory? A woman traveling alone would be ripe for the plucking. She'd have to travel at night and find secure shelter during the day. But the idea of traveling at night filled her with fear. Everything filled her with fear. She touched her belly. *Got to be strong.*

Within three days, they came to a river that had overflowed its banks, the water running wild and rapid.

Moon Magic danced and pawed, moving backwards instead of forward toward the river. He hadn't forgotten their last water crossing. Neither had she. She stroked his neck. "We gonna be fine, boy." Her words didn't calm him. Maybe he could hear the quiver in her voice.

Julia glanced at Wanbli, sitting calmly atop his horse. "How do we get across?"

"We ride."

Not again. Julia had barely gotten good with riding on solid ground. *But riding in the river with raging water and fallen trees?* She'd fall off the horse into the river lickety-split, just like she'd done before. "Can't we build a raft?"

"Not deep. Watch."

He dug his heels into the horse's midsection, urging the animal into the river.

When the two reached the middle, the water lapped at Wanbli's thighs. He reached the other side; then he turned and waved her on.

She swallowed hard against the lump in her throat.

The water was grey blue and moving swiftly, not the calm muddy brown of the bayou.

But she'd never get to Canada standing on this side of the river. Stroking Moon Magic's side, she whispered, "We can do this." She guided the horse into the water.

The river was frigid. It stole her breath and made her racing heart stutter. "Please, Lord. Help me and my baby this day. Place your hand upon us and guide us." She wanted to close her eyes and only open them when she reached the other side, but that would be foolhardy. She had to face her fears. Her child depended on her being brave.

Water splashed around her ankles and then climbed up her legs. Her teeth knocked together. The distance to where Wanbli stood wrapped in a blanket on the opposite bank seemed to grow. She looked behind her. Going back would take as long as going forward. She swallowed hard and tightened the hold on the horse's reins.

Moon Magic danced beneath her, the white of one eye showing large and his ears flattened against his water-soaked head.

Julia. She felt Trades with Horses calming presence, his courage. She loosened her grip on the reins, giving the horse its head.

The horse's weight shifted. He lengthened his sleek brown head, until the water was just below his jaw. Moon Magic was swimming.

She could get to the other side.

When they were a little ways from shore, Wanbli came out and guided her and Moon Magic to land.

Julia slid off the horse and dropped to her knees. She placed her lips on the muddy surface and kissed the ground.

Sunkawakan Iyopeya woke.

The wagon had stopped moving.

The trunk that lay across his stiff and cold body shifted. He held his breath.

Laughter.

"Father," one guard said, "when you're on the trail, you sleep in your clothes in case of attack."

"Really?" the old priest asked.

Silence.

"I'm just going to move the trunk, so I can find fresh clothes tomorrow after my morning bath."

"Let me help you, Father," one of the guards said.

"No, no, that—"

The weight of the trunk was lifted from Sunkawakan Iyopeya's body. He almost groaned.

"Thank you. Thank you," the old man said.

More laughter as the soldiers' voices faded away.

Someone patted his knee. "They will sleep shortly," the priest whispered.

Snores jerked Sunkawakan Iyopeya out of a restless doze.

He eased back the rough and scratchy blanket and peered out. Night had fallen, and the moon was hidden behind the clouds. He shifted and the wagon creaked. He froze.

"One guard is patrolling beyond the trees," Father Keegan whispered. His voice came from beneath the wagon.

Sunkawakan Iyopeya crept out and hunkered down by the rear wagon wheel. Only the priest's white hair could be seen above his blanket. Another guard slept by the fire.

The horses had been hobbled away from the wagon. He could not risk alerting the guards to his presence by taking one of the animals. He would have to make his way on foot.

"Thank you, Father," he whispered.

"Go with God, my son," came the soft response.

He crept into the trees. Nothing stirred—no predators, no owl. From his right came the crunch of boots on dried leaves. The soldier made so much noise he would not hear an enemy if they approached. He passed within touching distance of Sunkawakan Iyopeya's hiding place.

After the sentry had moved on, Sunkawakan Iyopeya crept out of the protection of the trees and faded into the darkness, moving deeper into the woods.

By the time the sun crested the hills, he had traveled much distance on foot from the priest and the soldiers.

On the third morning, he came upon two wild stallions. In his weakened state, he was grateful to capture the slowest.

Eight days later, he crested a hill and saw the winter camp still nestled in the protection of a stand of pine and naked maple trees.

He walked through the village toward his mother's teepee. Someone took his horse away. Others followed in his wake, pounding his back and shoulders in a sign of welcome and joy.

His mother peered out of her teepee, glaring at the people who surrounded her dwelling. When he stepped out of their midst, she blinked as though blinded by the sun. She collapsed in his arms and touched his cheek. "Is it really you?"

"Yes, Mother." He scanned the people who crowded around, but there was no brown- faced, honey-eyed woman. "Where is Julia?"

"She is gone."

He heard his mother's words, but he could make no meaning of what she said. "Gone? Gone where?"

His mother shrugged. Her disregard for the most important person in his life made the skin around his mouth tight. He stepped back so he could see the truth in her eyes.

"Gone where, Mother?" he asked again.

"She has gone to the North." Matosapa stepped out of the crowd. "She wanted to leave. I sent Wanbli with her to show her the way."

He could not speak. A thousand thoughts tumbled through his tired brain. Why would she leave? He remembered their last conversation. She had been angry because he would not take her with him into Fort Laramie. Did she leave because of that? Or did she leave because he did not protect her, did not honor her as a man would honor someone he loved?

He had to find her. He leapt on the back of the nearest horse, ready to charge out of the camp in search of her.

Matosapa grabbed the reins. "You are tired. Eat and sleep. If it is important to go after this woman, tomorrow will be soon enough."

He jerked the reins from the older man's hands, a show of disrespect. But the medicine man had made no effort to show Julia respect. Nor had his mother.

Had Matosapa ordered Chaske to kill Julia? Sunkawakan Iyopeya held the older man's gaze. Steady black eyes stared back at him. The man was a skilled diplomat—a mask hid his true feelings.

Sunkawakan Iyopeya searched for his sister in the crowd. If his mother and the medicine man lied and something had happened to Julia, it would be written on his sister's face. She was not as skilled at hiding her feelings.

Arms wrapped around her waist, she stood apart from his mother and the other tribal members. She moved through the crowd and touched his leg. "Matosapa is right. You will be rested in the morning. You can ride faster and longer." Her eyes flashed understanding. For the first time since they had become adults, he thought she did not hold malice in her heart toward him.

"Wanbli will keep her safe," she said.

At least three more hours of daylight remained. Hours that would put him closer to Julia. But his breath labored in his chest and pulled at the still inflamed flesh in his back.

He swung off his mount and surrendered the reins to one of the young men. "I will rest," he said to no one in particular. He needed to be whole when he found Julia.

He entered the warmth of the teepee he and Julia had built for his mother. She and the medicine man followed him. Meat roasted on the fire.

Before the flap had closed Matosapa asked, "What happened to Chaske?"

So the old man did not believe whatever Wanbli and Julia had told him. Sunkawakan Iyopeya had no doubt the medicine man had asked them about his son.

Delaying, he pulled his knife from his belt and cut a hunk of meat from the roasting carcass. Hot grease dripped over his fingers. He did not mind the pain. The pain took his mind off his best friend's betrayal.

He chewed slowly, wondering what Wanbli and Julia had said about Chaske.

"His death honored the Great Spirit." The lie made the meat bitter in his mouth. He met the medicine man's gaze. "Your son is where he belongs."

Matosapa studied him for a long heartbeat. "You are at a crossroads. Decide wisely the course you will take." The medicine man gathered his robes around him and strode out of the teepee.

No longer hungry, Sunkawakan Iyopeya tossed the tasteless meat into the flames. He wiped his hands on his pants.

"Why go after her?" His mother sat on the opposite side of the fire. "I knew this woman would cause trouble. She has divided the tribe."

"No," he said. "She has come between you and the medicine man's dreams." He said this not unkindly. His mother deserved his respect. She had birthed him.

"When I find Julia, we will leave this camp and seek shelter with another Sioux tribe."

That he would leave his father's people pained him.

His mother cried out as though he had ripped her heart from her chest. "You would be chief. Yet you throw this all away."

"I throw nothing away. I do not need to be chief. I only need her love and respect." He stood, his body stiff with the anger he felt towards his mother and the sadness of losing the connection with his family. "I will find other shelter tonight."

"Whoa." Julia pulled back on Moon Magic's reins. She took a deep breath. Even though she and Wanbli had traveled a distance from the river, she imagined she could still hear the water's roar.

Her shoulders slumped and her body felt like she'd worked many hours in the cane field. Swinging her leg over the horse's back, she slid to the ground. All she wanted to do was sleep. Two days might be enough.

The pounding of hooves vibrated beneath her feet. She'd wondered how long it would take Wanbli to realize she no longer rode behind him.

"Why do you stop?"

Ignoring him, she led her horse to a patch of new grass.

"There is much light left in the day."

She could hear the impatience in his voice. "I'm tired," she snapped. She pressed her forehead into Moon Magic's warm side. "I just need to rest."

He snorted. A soft thump sound as his feet hit the ground.

"Women," he muttered, softly but loud enough for her to hear. She didn't care if he was put out by her action. She wasn't in control any more. The child in her belly was— Trades with Horses' child.

Julia looked up in time to see the Indian fade into the surrounding woods.

"Good riddance." She grabbed her bedroll off the horse, wrapped the blanket around her body and sat on the ground with her back pressed up against a budding tree.

She woke to the smell of roasting meat. Shadows had started to gather in the woods. In the distance, the fading sun cast a red glow over the surrounding mountains and the rising moon appeared milky in the sky.

Wanbli squatted by a fire and two rabbits cooked over the flames. Julia stomach growled. The Indian looked in her direction.

"That smells good," she said, rising. Her legs and back were stiff from the awkward sleeping position, but the sight of food improved her mood.

He didn't reply but hacked off a chunk of the rabbit and passed it to her. She ate it quickly, licking her fingers, before reaching for another slice.

"How much longer before we reach the end of Sioux territory," she asked around bites of the meat.

"A day or two."

A chill rippled through her. She lowered the meat. The rabbit now tasted like dust in her mouth. How would she make it without him? Except for the coming child, Wanbli was her last link to Trades with Horses. She'd thought about this moment when freedom would be hers for months. Once rosy, her dreams of freedom were...were as gray as the approaching night.

Later curled into her blanket, she realized she could have left the Indian village at any time. Trades with Horses hadn't forcing her to stay. She stayed because she belonged with him.

When Julia awoke two mornings later, Wanbli was gone. She sensed it, even before she found the crude map he'd drawn and the rifle with its ammunition. He'd said his goodbyes the night before.

Tucking the map in a leather pouch at her waist, she prepared for her journey north. Rolling up her bedding, she tied it in place on Moon Magic's back.

Her gaze strayed back in the direction she'd traveled, as though she could see Trades with Horses' village. As though she could see him.

She placed a hand over her belly. She and her baby would be all alone on this journey.

Keeping the hills on her right as the map indicated and the gun across her lap, she and Moon Magic started off toward her first landmark.

CHAPTER SEVENTEEN

The sun peeked over the foothills, sending out rays that crept slowly across the land. Sunkawakan Iyopeya made his way to the creek but paused when the holy man came into view.

Matosapa, arms thrown wide as though catching the sun, chanted a prayer. Sunkawakan Iyopeya waited until the old man finished his communion with the spirits before continuing his trek down to the water.

The medicine man watched his approach. He studied Sunkawakan Iyopeya for a long moment before speaking. "Will you not put this woman aside?"

The fate of his tribe weighed heavy on his spirit, but the thought of not growing old with Julia made his heart even heavier. "I cannot. She is my other half."

Something shifted in the shadows of the old man's eyes. "Even if your vision were true, what could you, one man, do against the Great White Father's army?"

Sunkawakan Iyopeya had told the elders of his Sun Dance vision but never felt they believed him. Now he was certain the medicine man had had the same vision of what lay ahead for their people. If the holy man knew what would come and truly cared about the Sioux people, why did he put such restrictions on his support of Sunkawakan Iyopeya?

"I would organize all the tribes friendly to the people. We could strike against the white man before he destroyed us." It was too late to talk. The white man would only understand action. He knew of no other way of stopping them. They would not just go away. They had shown their intent by killing animals for sport and destruction of the land.

"The Great Spirit will lead us to victory," the medicine man said.

Sunkawakan Iyopeya believed in the Wakan Tanka—the Great Spirit—but more was needed to win against the white man. But no elder would elect him chief if he gave voice to this belief.

Why did he want so badly to be chief? Did he only want the glory of leading his people into battle, of being the one the people turned to in times of need? Was his spirit so small he needed others to build him up? No, it was more. He could not put it into words, but it was as though the Wakan Tanka had given him this vision to lead.

A smug smile played across the medicine man's face. He knew of the struggle inside Sunkawakan Iyopeya's heart.

"It is not too late," the old man said. "You can still be chief."

Yes, the medicine man knew of the struggle. And if he could, he would use this struggle to create distance between Sunkawakan Iyopeya and Julia.

Julia's face flashed before his mind's eye, her independent spirit, her courage, her love of him. "I can be chief without your support." His words were brave, even arrogant. He was not altogether certain he would be chosen without Matosapa behind him, but he would try to have both—Julia and the chiefdom.

The old man turned away and stared out over the river. The water captured his attention for so long, Sunkawakan Iyopeya thought he had forgotten their conversation— forgotten he was there. Finally the old medicine man straightened his shoulders, standing like the black bear for which he was named. He turned his attention back to

Sunkawakan Iyopeya. "We must all walk our heart's path and reap the harvest our actions have sowed." With that said, he turned and stalked up the trail to the camp.

It was the third evening without Wanbli. The day had been warmer, and Julia hadn't needed her blanket past midmorning. She reached the forked river and swung wearily off Moon Magic's back. She had made much progress that day, so when she spotted the river she was grateful. It was a signal to rest.

She leaned back against a large boulder, before placing her swollen feet in the cold river. A short distance away Moon Magic drank his fill from the clear stream. The rock had captured the warmth of the sun, and she enjoyed the heat at her back. The horse now nibbled at early green stalks of grass that peeked up out of the dark soil.

She felt at peace for the first time since she'd left the Indian camp. Not happy but at peace. She'd never be totally happy now Trades with Horses was dead, but when the baby came things would be better. She blocked from her thoughts how she would feed and raise a child. Time later for that worry.

Through heavy lids, she watched sunrays dance across the river. Moon Magic whinnied.

A doe watched her from the edge of the woods. She should hunt for dinner, but she was too tired. "Shh…" she said to her horse. "Everything will be okay."

She woke to the sight of a tall man blocking out the last of the day's light. Her heart jumped in her chest like a rabbit caught in a snare. Her feet clumsy and heavy from sleep refused to support her as she tried to scramble away.

"Julia." The vision spoke with Trades with Horses' voice. "It's me." The man moved toward her, hand extended.

Tears slid down her face. She was dreaming. But it was so real...so true.

Only when a branch cut deep into the flesh of her leg did she realize she wasn't dreaming. She tried to stand, stumbled, but the man caught her before she fell.

Now that the man had stepped forward out of the shadows cast by the fading sun, she could see a smile playing at the corner of his lips. He stroked her arms, his hand warm against her chilled skin. His gentle fingers moved slowly from her hands to her shoulders as though he were soothing a restless mare.

"You...you..." Her fingers skimmed over his smooth face. His skin was warm. "You're alive."

He drew her into his arms. "I'm alive."

She felt his heart beating steadily against her body, felt his lips pressed to the flesh just behind her ear. "How—what...?"

"Father Keegan saved me."

She pulled out of his arms and stared up at him. "The Catholic man? He was still there?"

"Not now. We left the fort together." Trades with Horses traced the edges of her face with his rough fingers. She knew he didn't understand the word love, but she knew that was the light blazing out of his eyes.

"Will you come back with me?" he asked. His eyes searched her face. "Back to my father's tribe?"

She closed her eyes and fought the pull of his gaze. She had to think wisely for her child. What would their life be like living with his people? Did he understand how much his mother and the medicine man hated her? Did he understand they might never accept her?

But the feeling of darkness and despair she'd felt when she thought he was dead swamped her. If she made it to Canada, she might live the rest of her life in freedom but her heart would be forever tied to this land, to this man.

"We will." She took his hand and placed it over her belly.

He frowned, staring down at his hand over her deerskin skirt. Then the lines on his face cleared, and he straightened his shoulders. "It will be difficult these years ahead, but I will keep you and our children safe."

"I know you will."

His gaze roamed over her features. What she saw shining out of his eyes was their future. A future of freedom. A future of love.

Thank you for purchasing Lakota Moon Rising. I hope you enjoyed it. Check out ***Lakota Dreaming***, a contemporary mystery whose main characters are Julia and Sunkawakan Iyopeya's descendants.

Constance Gillam
www.constancegillam.com
www.facebook.com/authorconstancegillam
Twitter: @conniegillam
www.pinterest.com/constancegillam

Made in the USA
Middletown, DE
08 March 2017